THE PLOT TO KILL HITLER
BOOK ONE
CONSPIRACY

ANDY MARINO

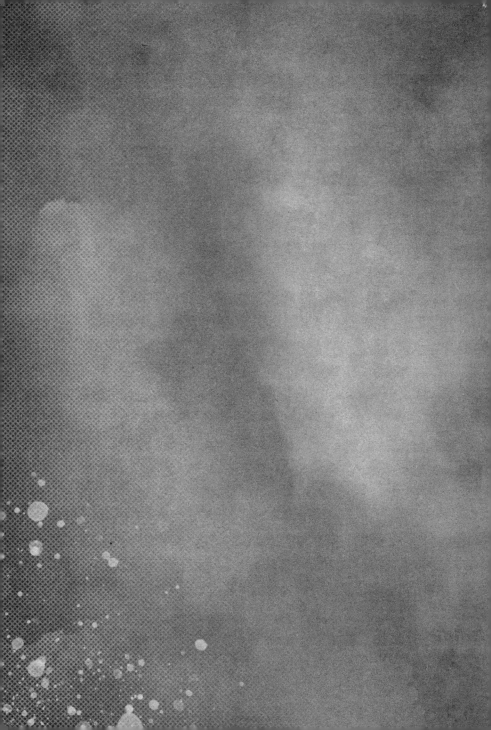

THE PLOT TO KILL HITLER

BOOK ONE

CONSPIRACY

ANDY MARINO

Scholastic Inc.

Copyright © 2020 by Andy Marino

All rights reserved. Published by Scholastic Inc., *Publishers since 1920*. SCHOLASTIC and associated logos are trademarks and/or registered trademarks of Scholastic Inc.

The publisher does not have any control over and does not assume any responsibility for author or third-party websites or their content.

No part of this publication may be reproduced, stored in a retrieval system, or transmitted in any form or by any means, electronic, mechanical, photocopying, recording, or otherwise, without written permission of the publisher. For information regarding permission, write to Scholastic Inc., Attention: Permissions Department, 557 Broadway, New York, NY 10012.

This book is a work of fiction. Names, characters, places, and incidents are either the product of the author's imagination or are used fictitiously, and any resemblance to actual persons, living or dead, business establishments, events, or locales is entirely coincidental.

ISBN 978-1-338-35902-2

10 9 8 7 6 5 4 3 2 1   20 21 22 23 24

First edition, April 2020

Printed in the U.S.A.   40

Book design by Christopher Stengel

For Mark

ONE

The all-clear signal screamed across the city of Berlin. Its single sharp note was a welcome change from the eerie howl of the air-raid warning siren.

Max Hoffmann, his sister, Gerta, and his mutti and papa emerged from their cellar. While Max lit the living room's lamp, its bulb filtered blue according to the rules enforced by the neighborhood *luftschutzwart*—air-raid warden—Gerta gave a sudden cry of alarm. Papa froze in place, a portly silhouette in the doorway to the kitchen. Mutti gripped her husband's arm.

Max blinked. He felt like his thoughts were moving slowly, out of sync with his family. The night's air raid had come perilously close to the Berlin district of Dahlem, where the Hoffmanns' neat villa sat nestled at the end of a leafy street. His head throbbed with the lingering echoes of the bombs, dropped from the bellies of the British Royal Air Force Avro

Lancasters that had blanketed the night sky. The flak fire from Berlin's air defense towers—monstrous 128-millimeter guns sending up great explosive cloudbursts—only added to the gut-rattling cacophony. And so it took Max a moment to separate the sound that had caught his sister's attention from the blasts still ringing in his ears.

"Someone's at the door," Gerta whispered.

Max's face reddened. He was grateful for the blackout so that Gerta couldn't see him flush. While it was Gerta's job to turn off the villa's water, gas, and electricity at the beginning of a raid, it was Max's job to open the doors and windows. This was part of the official air-raid procedure all across the city—opening doors and windows kept the pressure waves caused by bomb blasts from taking down entire buildings.

Maybe the wind slammed the door shut, Max thought. It was November, after all—and a bitter one at that.

Papa pushed his spectacles up the bridge of his nose, gently removing Mutti's fingers from his arm. He brushed plaster dust from the front of his rumpled shirt and went to the door. There he stood for a moment, listening, hand poised on the doorknob.

KNOCK KNOCK KNOCK

Max's father peered into the peephole.

A muffled voice came through the door. *"Herr Hoffmann. Bitte!"*

Max pictured a surly air-raid warden accompanied by a pair of grim SS storm troopers. Maybe the sandbags hadn't been properly secured, and light from the grates had caught the all-seeing eyes of the neighborhood's fanatical Nazis, so quick to denounce their neighbors for the slightest infractions. Repeat offenders even had their homes plastered in big, eye-catching signs designed to inflict maximum shame:

Dieses Haus ist schlecht verdunkelt!

(This house is poorly blacked out!)

But instead of muttering a curse and slowly opening the door to accept an official scolding, Karl Hoffmann flung it open with a look of alarm. He glanced back at his family and called for help.

Gerta and Mutti sprang into action, but Max was rooted to the floor by a brief glimpse of the figure outside. Staggering out of a nightmare of ash and smoke, the stranger was covered in blood.

He was a young man, tall and lean, with a jagged gash cruelly sliced into the side of his head. His face was a mask of blood, gleaming darkly—almost jet-black—in the blue-filtered lamplight.

A chill wind swirled in at his back, icy fingers plucking the unruly strands of Max's hair.

Numbly, Max stepped aside as Mutti and Papa carried the limp stranger into the kitchen, slumped across their shoulders.

Gerta slammed the front door shut, but it was too late—the damp November chill had crept in like an insidious spell.

Max met his sister's eyes in the gloom. Before he could ask if she had any idea who that man was or why he was here, Papa was calling for him.

"Max, we need light in here, please."

Karl Hoffmann's voice remained soft, measured, and patient, even when the rest of the world seemed to be frantically spinning off its axis. It was this grace under pressure that made him an indispensable surgeon, tending to the many thousands of Berlin's injured and afflicted civilians, from the bomb-ravaged to the disease-infected to the malnourished.

"Yes, Papa." Max rushed into the kitchen, where his parents were carefully laying the man out upon the kitchen table. It wasn't quite long enough for his lanky frame, and his arms and legs dangled off the edges. Max fumbled about in the drawer full of candles and matches, wondering if he would ever be able to eat at the table again without thinking of blood soaking the wood.

"Ach, Maxi," Mutti said, "just bring in the—"

"I've got it," Gerta said, accompanied by a dim blue glow. She set the living room lamp down on the counter next to the sink.

"Over here, please," Papa said, waving a hand above the

man's chest. Gerta brought the lamp over to the kitchen table and held it up as high as she could. As if the light itself had prodded his wounds, the man groaned in pain.

Now illuminated, Max noticed that the man's overcoat was in tatters, and the shirt underneath was in no better shape. With steady hands, his father gripped the center of the man's shirt and ripped it open. The man gave a strangled cry. His chest rose and fell with his rapid breathing, and his bare skin was slick with blood.

Light-headed, Max turned away.

"Max," Papa said, "I need you to get my bag from the study."

Grateful for a reason to leave the kitchen, Max scurried through the living room, past the bathroom, and into his father's cozy study, which smelled of the citrus cleaning solution Papa used to polish the desk. Even years after strict wartime rationing made such luxuries impossible to find, his father had always found a way. The black leather bag with its twin handles was in its right place, a snug cubbyhole beneath the desk.

Before the war, Papa had brought the bag with him when he made house calls to wealthy patients in Dahlem and Zehlendorf, and in the stately row houses of Charlottenburg. These days, Papa carried his bag to streets where entire apartment blocks had been reduced to rubble by a direct hit from an RAF bomb, or gutted from the inside out by the spread of a blaze sparked by an incendiary weapon.

Back in the kitchen, the stranger had taken a turn for the worse. He was shaking his head from side to side and muttering what sounded, to Max, like utter nonsense.

Max handed the bag to his father. His mother dipped a cloth into one of the buckets they'd filled with water and placed around the house, in case they had to put out a fire in a hurry. Mutti mopped blood from the man's brow. She did not flinch when he cried out. At the same time, Gerta held the lamp with unwavering concentration while Papa rummaged through his bag until he came up with several morphine syrettes—needles with a little tube at the end that you squeezed, like toothpaste, instead of using a plunger.

For a moment it looked as if the Hoffmanns were posing for a painting, lit by dramatic blue-tinted light and deep shadow. Strangely, Max was struck by how *normal* the scene felt to him. Before the war, it would have been unthinkable for his father to let him witness even a minor medical operation. But lately, as the RAF bombings sent thousands of Berliners scrambling into their cellars, and the air-raid sirens turned from nuisances to harbingers of fire and blood, Max's father had quietly enlisted the help of each member of the Hoffmann family.

There had been no earnest conversation about their new

responsibilities. No family meeting. That was not his father's way. Instead, Max and his sister had simply found themselves pitching in, following their father's example, helping tend to the wounded as they were carted out of apartments with walls blown to pieces but rooms very much intact, like giant crumbling dollhouses. Max had taken note of his mother's wartime activities, too—watching as she secretly delivered bits of bread and cheese to *ostarbeiter*, the foreign workers from conquered nations forced to clear rubble until their backs gave out.

"Is he a neighbor, Papa?" Gerta asked.

Max saw the briefest flicker pass across Mutti's face as she met Papa's eyes.

Papa shook his head. "He was out in the street during the raid. Look."

Gerta leaned in fearlessly. Max took a deep breath and moved closer to the table. He would not let his sister be the brave one while he skulked in the shadows.

There was a peculiar smell coming from the stranger, which Max quickly realized was actually the mingling of several familiar war smells—acrid smoke mixed with metal, and the earthy, rusty tang that meant *blood*.

Papa's hand hovered over a gash in the man's chest that ran from his collarbone to his stomach. Just below his belly button, a twist of metal like a spiky corkscrew stuck out.

Max felt his dinner of turnip soup and ersatz bread—mostly

made of sawdust—roil his stomach. He glanced at his sister, whose face mimicked the clinical detachment of their father's, and pulled himself together.

"This is shrapnel from an antiaircraft shell," Papa said, pointing at the corkscrew.

"He was caught in the steel hail," Mutti said. Max knew what she meant: the pitter-patter of exploded metal bits that rained down on their roof during a raid, when the flak guns defending Berlin opened up and dark cloudbursts filled the skies.

Suddenly, the man stopped writhing. He steadied himself, began to speak, stopped, and began again. His voice was low and hoarse, but now, at least, his words made sense.

"Look in the pocket of my overcoat, Herr Hoffmann."

Carefully, Papa reached into the half-shredded pocket and removed a neat bundle of folded papers secured with twine.

Max longed for his father to give some indication of how he knew this man, but Papa's face was impassive. His mother wrung out the cloth on the floor next to the table, dipped it in the bucket, and resumed gently washing the stranger's face.

Papa placed the bundle of papers in his doctor's bag. He did not undo the twine or betray the slightest curiosity about the papers' contents. He simply glanced at his wife and nodded. Mutti bent a little closer to the man and began to softly sing.

Good evening, good night
With roses covered,
With cloves adorned,
Slip under the covers.

Gerta reached out for Max, and instead of pulling away in his usual half-mocking brotherly disgust, he held her hand. The song was "Brahms's Lullaby," and Max and Gerta knew it well. Mutti had sung it to them when they were very little, drifting off to sleep in their apartment in Neukölln. This was long before their father's promotion to head of the trauma surgery at the university hospital, and their move to the villa in Dahlem. Long before the war.

Max watched Papa break the seal on one of the syrettes, sink the needle into the flesh of the man's thigh, and flatten the tube.

The man closed his eyes, and a smile played at his trembling lips.

Then, suddenly, he seemed to fight against the calming tide of the morphine flooding his bloodstream. He came abruptly to life and struggled to sit up, as if waking from an uneasy dream. But Mutti pressed his shoulders down to keep him lying flat. His dangling arm shot up, and Max jumped back, startled.

The man's hand gripped Papa's, and he pulled Karl Hoffmann down toward him until their faces were nearly touching.

"For the sake of humanity," he said in an astonishingly clear voice, "the Führer must die. Finish it, Karl!"

Stunned, Max turned to his father and watched as Papa met the man's eyes. He gave an almost imperceptible nod. Then the man's entire body seemed to deflate. He let go of Papa's hand and fell still.

Max swallowed. His throat was as dry as the sawdust in the ersatz bread. He had just watched a man die on their kitchen table.

His heart was pounding so hard he thought the whole neighborhood would be able to hear it. He glanced at his sister. Gerta didn't have to say a word—Max knew they were both wondering the same thing.

The Führer must die . . .

Was their father plotting to kill Adolf Hitler?

TWO

In his bedroom on the second floor of the villa, Max sifted through his collection of wooden miniatures, which had been knocked off their shelf. His uncle Friedrich had whittled the knights, horses, pikemen, catapults, and other medieval figures from blocks of wood and given them to Max for him to paint. He had managed to finish only a handful of them before the war. His set of tiny brushes, which could detail the pupil of an eye with pinpoint accuracy, sat useless and unused in the drawer of his small desk. There were no tubes of paint to be had—everything the city's factories churned out, from paints to the soles of shoes to safety pins—supplied the Nazi war machine. The ordinary citizens of Berlin were left to fight over black-market scraps.

"Maybe you should glue them to the shelf," Gerta said, appearing in his doorway.

In tonight's raid, bombs had fallen close enough to rumble

the earth around the foundation of their house. Max imagined that his room had been like a snow globe, violently shaken, then left to settle. Now it looked even messier than usual, with miniatures scattered across the floor. His soccer cleats were nowhere to be found, and a plate he'd stupidly left on the dresser was now a mess of jagged shards between his bed and the door.

"Careful!" Max said as Gerta stepped into his room. He winced as she crunched little bits of porcelain with every step.

"First rule of air raids: Wear shoes," she said.

"You're trying to make Herr Siewert proud, I see."

Franz Siewert was their neighborhood air-raid warden. He was also the *blockwart*—the block warden responsible for keeping eyes and ears on his neighbors and reporting any suspicious behavior to his Nazi Party superiors.

In the Hoffmann family, there was an ongoing and spirited debate over who hated Herr Siewert the most. Max was sure it was him—the *blockwart* stuffed himself into a brown uniform that was one size too small, and his beady eyes gave Max the creeps. Plus, he was really just a grown-up version of a tattletale.

"Blech," Gerta said. "Don't speak his name aloud in this house, please."

She sat down on Max's bed, made a face, stood up, and plucked a small wooden figure from the bedspread.

"I didn't know you had a queen," she said.

"Beatrice!" Max exclaimed, snatching the miniature from her hand. "I was looking for her everywhere." He placed the queen carefully up on the shelf next to a king with an oversized gold crown that glinted eerily in the blue-tinted light.

The raid was over. By now, the bombers would be returning to their bases in England, but the city's air-raid rules stated that as long as it was still dark outside, the blackout must remain in effect.

Gerta raised an eyebrow. She seemed about to say something, then shook her head and went to the doorway. She leaned out into the hall and listened for a moment. There were voices downstairs. Two men, Max thought. More strangers.

Gerta shut the bedroom door.

"Okay, little brother," she said quietly. "We need to talk about the man in our kitchen."

Max closed his eyes and fought back a wave of nausea. He had been alarmingly close to throwing up from the minute the man crossed their threshold, and he didn't want to do it in his bedroom. Especially not in front of his sister.

"You can't just pretend this isn't happening," Gerta said.

Yes, I can, Max wanted to say—*watch me!* The bombing raids had forced him to become an expert at pretending life was completely normal. At night he huddled in the cellar while death rained down from the fiery sky; in the morning he walked to school down a sidewalk pitted with craters, past piles of rubble that used to be Meyer's Candy Store and the Cinema Français.

Berlin was a city that swept up and got on with it, and it was impossible for Max not to soak up some of that attitude.

Besides, he really did not want to think about the dead man in the kitchen.

"Max," Gerta said.

Reluctantly, he opened his eyes. She was standing with her arms folded.

A loud *thump* came from downstairs. Max swallowed. "What are they doing?"

"It's two orderlies from the hospital that Papa trusts. They're helping him move the body."

Max grimaced. *The body.* His vision swam. "To where?" he asked weakly.

Gerta shrugged. "Not here, anyway. So that's good news."

Max held up a knight whose silver armor he was especially proud of. "Do you think he should be guarding the king or the queen?"

Gerta snatched the knight from his hand. "Don't change the subject."

She set the miniature on the shelf next to the king, then took a step closer to Max. "That man went outside during a bombing raid just to deliver those papers to Papa," Gerta said. "I think that was very brave."

Max frowned. During the sporadic, lighter bombing raids of 1941 and 1942, it had become something of a spectator sport to go outside and watch the action—the flak bursting like popcorn, the searchlights piercing the darkness to trap bombers in webs of light, the orange glow of incendiary fires across the city—but November of 1943 brought a new reckoning down upon Berlin. Where the RAF had once seemed half-hearted, it now seemed focused and committed, sending thousands of long-range bombers to strike the heart of the German capital. Walking the streets during one of these massive raids was suicide.

"Why would anybody go outside in that?" Max asked.

Gerta rolled her eyes. "Because it's the perfect cover! Even the Gestapo inspectors are hiding in basement shelters on a night like tonight."

"Right," Max said, as if he'd already thought of that. "So whatever's in those papers must be really important."

Gerta's eyes flashed. "Which is why we need to see what it is."

"Yeah, but—"

"They're probably still in Papa's bag."

"They're tied up with string. He'll know if we untie it."

"We'll figure out how to tie it back up! This is important,

Max. You heard what the man said. *The Führer must die.* If Papa's involved in . . ." She lowered her voice, a reflex for any Berliner, even in the relative safety of their homes, as they were constantly surrounded by eavesdropping busybodies eager to denounce their neighbors as enemies of the Nazi regime. ". . . *assassination,* then I think we deserve to know."

Max looked down at his scattered miniatures with a sudden pang of longing for the Hoffmanns' Sunday dinners. Before the war, Uncle Friedrich would bring a new wooden figure every week. Papa would fetch a bottle of wine from the cellar, Mutti would cook pork schnitzel . . . and now, Uncle Friedrich was off fighting the Soviets, the cellar was a makeshift air-raid shelter, and there was very little pork to be had.

Max scooped up an armored horse and a court jester and arranged them on the shelf. *Pick up the pieces, get some sleep, go to school in the morning.* Someday soon, Uncle Friedrich would return from the Eastern Front, the empty shelves in the grocery stores would fill up again, and life in Berlin would go back to normal. Better to keep hope in his thoughts than worry himself sick over the man in the kitchen and shadowy assassination plots. That was how a person went crazy.

"What if I don't want to know?" Max said.

Gerta put her hands on her hips and regarded him severely. "What does Mutti say about Berliners?"

Max sighed. "That they stick their heads in the sand like

ostriches so they don't have to see what's going on around them."

"Which is?"

"People being taken from their homes and relocated."

"What kind of people?"

"Jewish people. And anybody who speaks out against the Nazis."

"And what does 'relocated' really mean?"

Max sat down on the bed. His vision swam. "Relocated" meant taken by third-class train to new settlements in Poland and Hungary—everybody said so. He wished Gerta would leave him alone so he could put his room back together and get some sleep. There was going to be an arithmetic test in the morning. Long division. He needed to study. He needed to—

"It means *killed*, Max," Gerta said, answering her own question. "*Relocated* really means *murdered by the Nazis*."

Max closed his eyes. His thoughts churned. The reason everybody "hid like ostriches" was because they didn't want to get a late-night visit from the Gestapo and suffer the same fate as their "relocated" neighbors.

"If Papa really is involved in some kind of plot," Max said, his voice near a whisper, "then isn't it better for us not to know the details, in case we're questioned?"

Gerta folded her arms and cocked her head. "Clever trick, Maxi." A smile threatened to break out on her face. "Okay, fine! Make up your own mind about what you want to know and what you don't."

More muffled voices drifted up from downstairs. Max heard the door to the backyard open and close.

"But I need to know," Gerta said, crunching porcelain on her way out of his room.

Max sat alone on his bed for a moment, thinking. Then he got up and followed his sister down the hall. "Gerta!" he whispered. "Wait up!"

THREE

Max crept downstairs at his sister's heels. There was seldom silence in the wake of a raid—especially one that had hit so close—but even the shrill sirens of the fire brigades and the shouted orders of the rescue crews seemed like blissful peace after hours of earth-shaking thunder.

Max and Gerta peeked into the kitchen. Mutti was scrubbing the table and did not spare them a glance. They moved down the hall, stepping carefully over a silver sconce that had been jolted from its perch on the wall, its candle nowhere to be seen. It was very dark in the hallway, and Max wondered if the day would come when their electricity would be completely lost. Then even their dim, blue-filtered lamps would be useless. They would have to paint their floors and walls with white phosphorescent paint, like the curbs and sidewalks of the city. His classmate Joseph had told Max that in the public shelter near Friedrichstrasse Station there was a wall of this glowing paint bright enough to read a newspaper by.

Gerta opened the door to their father's study. Max breathed in the faint odor of citrus. Gerta shut the door behind them and clicked on a small battery-powered torchlight. She swept the beam through the darkness, and Max thought of the searchlights on the flak towers. The powerful lamps would send cones of light up into the sky for the rest of the night until they faded into a gray, smoky dawn.

He felt his way to the cubbyhole beneath his father's desk. Empty.

"Gerta," he whispered. "The bag's not here." He wasn't sure if what he felt was relief, exactly, but he was fine with their little adventure ending before it could begin. You would think you would emerge from the cellar after an air raid with boundless energy, after being cooped up for hours. But it didn't work that way. Max always felt drained.

"Maybe it's back in the kitchen," Gerta said.

"No, Papa always puts it back here when he's done. That means he still has it with him."

"That doesn't make sense," Gerta said. "Those papers are too important for him to be walking around the streets with."

"How do you know?" Max said. "Maybe it's just a . . . a . . . schnitzel recipe."

Gerta snorted. Max followed the skinny beam of her torch

as it illuminated a corner of the rug. "What's that?" she asked, wiggling the light for emphasis.

Max shrugged. "The carpet?"

"No, dummy." She walked over to the corner of the room and knelt down. There was a small triangular piece of carpet sticking up into the air, as if it had been pulled from the floor like the tab on a tin of sardines. *"That."*

Gerta began to pull on the stray bit of carpet.

"Gerta . . . ," Max said. But then she lifted a precise square of the carpet along with the "tab," and Max's curiosity got the better of him. He crouched down next to his sister. Her torch revealed a shiny steel panel. Set into the metal was a numbered dial.

"It's a safe," Max said after a moment.

"My brother, the boy genius," Gerta said. She bent her ear close to the floor safe and slowly turned the dial.

Max knew that his sister was thinking of *Hornet and Wasp*, the radio serial broadcast by the BBC in England. It was against the law for Berliners to listen to foreign broadcasts, but everybody Max knew did it anyway, sometimes huddled with their radios under the sheets so they could listen at the lowest possible volume.

In the last episode of *Hornet and Wasp*, Hornet cracked a safe by using a doctor's stethoscope to listen to the nearly inaudible clicks as he turned the dial.

There was a stethoscope in Max's father's bag. That would do them no good. But maybe there was a spare instrument somewhere else in the study. The cabinets were full of medical equipment.

"Give me your torch," Max said.

"Shhhh!" Gerta hissed.

"Hornet had a stethoscope," Max pointed out.

"He also had a quiet partner," Gerta said. Then she raised her head from the safe. "Oh, forget it." She let the square of carpet fall back into place.

"Oh well," Max said, smoothing the patch until it looked completely undisturbed.

"At least now we know about Papa's hiding place," Gerta said.

"Uh-huh," Max said wearily. He knew that Gerta was just getting started. She would blow the safe open with dynamite if she had to.

Suddenly, a floorboard creaked just outside the door to the study. Max froze. Gerta clicked off her torch.

The door opened, and Mutti walked into the study and lit the lamp. She turned and gave a startled yelp at the sight of Max and Gerta standing in the dark corner of the room. She put her hand against her heart and caught her breath.

"My God, I thought you were in bed! What are you doing creeping around like cat burglars? You have school in the morning, and it's almost two!"

Max felt himself relax. He liked it when his mother fussed about getting to bed. It reminded him of the years before the war, when the only things on his mind were soccer games at recess and whether he would have fresh potato pancakes with sour cream and applesauce for lunch.

"I guess nobody told the Royal Air Force it was a school night," Gerta said.

Mutti gave Gerta a pointed look. "We are all still alive. Our house is still standing. We are more fortunate than many others. This family does not use hardship as an excuse when so many others have it much worse."

"Like the man who came to deliver papers to Papa." Gerta was intractable tonight.

"Gerta . . . ," Max said. Another wave of nausea hit him. He had been so close to getting through the rest of the night without thinking about the dead man in the kitchen.

Mutti stepped toward them. Her voice softened. "I'm sorry you had to see that. But you know Papa—he is bound by duty and his oath as a surgeon to help anyone in need. We couldn't have turned him away. You understand. And I want you to know that you were both very brave."

Max noted that his mother did not mention the papers, despite the purposeful way that Gerta brought them up.

A noise like distant thunder rattled Max's guts. An unexploded incendiary, probably triggered by the fire brigade. The sound wrenched him back to the moment Papa opened the door. Max relived the moments that followed as a series of images.

The gash in the man's face.

The light in his eyes going out as the morphine swept him away.

The Führer must die.

"Max?" His mother's voice sounded far away, like it was drifting up to him from the bottom of a deep well. He felt her palm on his shoulder, and then the back of her hand brushed his cheek.

His memory paused on his father reaching into the leather bag. Again, he saw Papa calmly inject the morphine into the man's thigh. Papa had not used any of the instruments from his bag, or even attempted to give the man care. He had simply helped him float away . . .

The walls of the study came rushing back. Max found himself looking into his mother's eyes.

"Oh, Maxi," she said. "Let it out. It's okay."

He felt his eyes well up with tears. He did not want to cry in front of Gerta, but he did not know if he could hold back.

"Papa didn't save him," he said. "He didn't even try."

"Sometimes, your father knows right away that nothing can be done," Mutti said. "All he could do was ease the man's pain."

Max nodded. Next to him, he could sense that his sister was coiled like a spring—she wanted desperately to bring up the papers, but was biting her tongue.

Mutti embraced them both. "Now get some sleep," she said. "Tomorrow the sun will shine."

FOUR

The next day, the sun did shine—in patches, at least, through gaps in the greasy smoke that lingered over the city.

After school, Max and Gerta joined their parents to help clear rubble from Königin-Luise-Strasse, a few blocks from their villa. A nearby explosion had reduced the facade of an apartment building to a pile of brick that cascaded down over the sidewalk and into the street.

Somewhere, buried in the rubble, a telephone rang.

Max and Gerta hefted larger bricks as a team, plunking them into waiting wheelbarrows to be carted away by sunken-cheeked *ostarbeiter*. Max watched his mother slip a ration coupon from her pocket and approach one of the foreign work details. Just before she reached them, Papa grabbed her arm and pulled her back. Puzzled, Max glanced around. And then he cursed under his breath.

"Here comes the pig," he muttered to Gerta.

The *blockwart* strutted along the edge of the rubble, an unlit cigar jammed into the corner of his mouth. As usual, he wore his Nazi-issued brown uniform, and his boots were perfectly shined.

He stopped when he reached the Hoffmanns and took a moment to survey the scene. He pulled the cigar from his mouth.

"Heil Hitler," he said sharply.

"Good afternoon, Herr Siewert," Mutti replied. Max winced. By not returning the standard German greeting of *Heil Hitler,* Mutti risked provoking the *blockwart.* All it would take was a single phone call from Franz Siewert, and the Gestapo would be paying the Hoffmanns a visit. Max thought of the dead man's papers, and Papa's floor safe . . .

"Heil Hitler," Papa said without enthusiasm.

Suddenly, Siewert reached out with a meaty hand and patted Max on the head. It took all of Max's willpower not to shrink away in disgust.

"Your dedication is impressive," Siewert said to Papa. "But surely there is no need to involve one so young in this operation."

"I'm twelve," Max said.

"And wouldn't a boy of twelve rather be playing with the proper friends? You know . . ." Siewert knelt down to speak to Max, eye to eye. Max could smell the stale tobacco of the unlit cigar on his breath. "Our magnificent organization, the German Youngsters in the Hitler Youth, fields many teams of great quality. A boy strong enough to lift these stones might find himself very useful on the soccer pitch."

"The bombs make no distinction between the old and the young, or the rich and the poor," Mutti said. "Neither should the rescue efforts. We are all Berliners."

Siewert looked at Mutti with distaste. "I am sure today's rescue effort will not miss one boy of twelve," he said. Then he glanced at Gerta. "Or one girl of thirteen."

Chills ran down Max's spine. If Siewert knew his and Gerta's exact ages, what else did he know about the Hoffmann family?

"I'll think about it," Max said.

Siewert nodded crisply. "Good boy. And don't worry about all this." He waved his hand vaguely over the rubble, as if casting a spell on it. "We have plenty of foreign laborers, and more are arriving every day, faster than we can process them. There is no need to waste the energies of German boys and girls on work that can be done by Gypsies and Poles." With that, Siewert stood up and popped the cigar back into his mouth.

"Herr Siewert," Papa said before the *blockwart* strode away. "One question for you, if I may."

"Of course, *herr doktor.*"

Papa nodded politely. "I was wondering if Herr Göring had changed his name yet."

Gerta snickered under her breath. Siewert stared blankly for a moment, and Max was worried that his father had taken it too far. Hermann Göring was the Nazi minister of aviation. Göring had been so confident in Germany's air defense system, he claimed that, "If one enemy bomber reaches Berlin, my name is not Göring, it's Meyer."

Papa always kept his mouth shut around Nazi officials—it was Mutti who liked to poke and prod at their serious, puffed-up demeanors. This was highly unusual. His father must be in a strange mood, and Max wondered if the events of last night had anything to do with it.

Slowly, Siewert pulled the cigar from his mouth. He took one step toward Papa, scowling, then stopped. He glanced at the ruined apartment building. Then he shook his head, and a rueful smile broke out on his face.

He pointed at Papa with the tip of the cigar. "I appreciate that, *herr doktor*. We Berliners must keep our sense of humor during times like these."

Papa smiled. "Heil Hitler," he said.

Herr Siewert looked pleased. He gave a crisp Nazi salute—right arm straight and angled upward, palm down—then marched off to berate a stooped old *ostarbeiter* as the man struggled with a wheelbarrow piled high with bricks.

Somewhere, the telephone was still ringing.

FIVE

omething's going on with them," Gerta said. She picked up the armored knight from Max's shelf, paced over to the bed, then back to the shelf, where she plunked the knight down next to the queen.

"Mutti and Papa?" Max asked. He slid his curtain aside and looked out at dusk settling over their little corner of Dahlem. Soon, the Hoffmanns would douse the lights completely in favor of the dim blue filters. He was so used to the weird hue by now that it tinted his dreams at night, and he often jolted awake, sweating and breathless, from blue-filtered nightmares.

"No," Gerta said, "Hitler and Mussolini. *Yes*, little brother, Mutti and Papa."

"I've never seen Papa act like that around Sie—around you-know-who. Pushing his buttons, I mean."

"Exactly," Gerta said.

Max let his eyes go slack. The villas across the street blurred into the salmon-colored November dusk, giving the neighboring houses the dreamy look of a watercolor wash.

Mutti had once told him that Adolf Hitler was a failed painter, and often—especially in the aftermath of yet another bombing raid—Max wondered what would have happened if Hitler had stuck with art instead of turning to Fascist political rabble-rousing. Would this entire war have been avoided? Would the Nazis, with their jackboots and their *heils* and their terrifying nighttime rallies, never have existed at all?

In that case, Berlin would be whole, undamaged by bombs, and thousands of its citizens would be home, enjoying their peaceful lives, instead of being "relocated." He imagined the ruins of the Cinema Français rising from the rubble, the bricks putting themselves back together, letters jumping up onto the marquee . . .

"Yoo-hoo," Gerta said, waving a hand in front of Max's face. He snapped out of his reverie. "I was saying, we need a plan."

"For what?"

"Dinner! We need to work together to find out what's going on."

"I think if they wanted us to know," Max said carefully, "they would have already told us." Why must Gerta push everything to the absolute limit! His brain was filled to the brim with worry and anxiety. The last thing he needed was another secret to keep, another task that made him feel too grown-up. He didn't want to feel grown-up. He hated to admit it, but the stupid *blockwart* was right—he *did* want to play soccer with his friends instead of joining the rescue efforts. Even playing on a Hitler Youth team didn't sound so bad. After all, they had real uniforms . . .

Gerta scowled. "It's not like Mutti and Papa to keep secrets from us. I don't like this one bit."

Max refrained from pointing out that they had just discovered Papa's secret floor safe in his study, and there was no telling how many more of their parents' secrets were undiscovered. Max knew that his sister's mind worked like a switchboard operator's. If she wasn't at the center of all incoming and outgoing Hoffmann-family information, it drove her crazy.

He sighed. "Fine, Gerta." He thought hard, trying to come up with a way to make Mutti and Papa let them in on whatever was going on. He looked around his room, his gaze sweeping across the stained-glass lamp on his dresser, the poster of the 1936 Summer Olympics, the shelf full of miniature knights and medieval royalty. Then he jumped up and grabbed the king from his place of honor.

"I've got an idea," he said. Gerta eyed the miniature figurine skeptically. But as Max told her his plan, a smile crept across her face.

"My brother, the boy genius," she said. This time, she meant it.

SIX

For Berliners, the wartime food rationing system worked like this: German citizens were divided into categories based on the physical demands of their work. An office clerk was a "normal consumer," a factory employee a "heavy worker," and a house builder a "very heavy worker." Then each citizen was issued color-coded ration cards that could be exchanged for meat, cheese, sugar, flour, rice, bread, tea, oatmeal, and other items, with the amounts determined by the citizen's category.

The rationing system was supposed to keep everyone from starving.

It did not always work.

Even if you had a blue ration card that allowed for 650 grams of meat per week, it did not mean you could actually get it—stores had shortages all the time, and often there was little to go around. It was such a problem that Mutti sometimes waited in grocery-store lines for several hours, only to come home empty-handed.

Still, as Mutti liked to remind Max and Gerta, the Hoffmanns had it better than most. Because Papa's work as a surgeon was so valuable to the health and morale of the people of Berlin, he had been classified as a "very heavy worker," which meant that the family was given the most generous food allotment.

Tonight, there was a loaf of real bread, not the dry, crumbly ersatz stuff made from sawdust. And Mutti had managed to get enough beef to make a hearty stew, complete with potatoes and some carrots and celery from her kitchen garden. Max's stomach rumbled as he sat down across from Gerta. He took in the savory smells as Papa cut the bread into thick slices.

"This looks wonderful, Ingrid," Papa said. "You are a true artist."

"Perhaps we should taste it before declaring me an artist," Mutti said. "I'm not entirely sure that Bremmer's didn't sell me horse meat instead of beef."

Max's stomach turned. Mutti saw the look on his face and grinned. "I'm kidding, Maxi. I only ever served you horse meat that one time."

Max racked his brain. Surely he would remember eating *horse*, right?

Papa chimed in slyly. "See? You didn't even know the difference."

Gerta burst out laughing. Max shook his head and ladled piping-hot stew into his bowl. "Very funny, everybody."

The stew was so tasty, Max quickly forgot about horse meat. The constant shortages gave everybody ravenous appetites, and it wasn't uncommon for the Hoffmanns to eat without saying a word to one another. Max was entirely focused on his meal, ripping off hunks of bread and dragging them through the sauce that clung to the bowl. It was only after they all sat back in their chairs with full bellies and Papa lit his pipe that Max caught Gerta's eye.

She gave him a slight nod. He pulled the figure of the king from his pocket and plunked it down on the table in front of him.

"Who's this, Maxi?" Mutti said.

"This is Adolf Hitler," Max said.

Mutti's mouth dropped open. Papa pulled the pipe stem from his mouth and coughed. Mutti quickly recovered her composure and fixed Max with a steely glare. "And what, pray tell, is he doing at our table?"

"Remember back in the spring," Max said, "when you told me that Hitler was going completely mad? So mad that he thought of himself as a medieval king?"

"Hmm. I suppose I might have said something like that."

Max shook his head. "You said it for a reason—*Sippenhaft.*"

"The blood laws," Gerta said. "Remember? After they tried to kill Hitler back in March, he made it a law that anybody involved in assassination plots would be killed—along with their entire families. Just like kings used to do."

"What are you two getting at?" Papa asked. He stared intently through his spectacles, first at Gerta, then at Max.

Max shifted uncomfortably under his father's gaze. Once you knew a secret, there was no going back. No way to unknow it.

"We were wondering . . ." He trailed off, gazing into his empty bowl as if he found it suddenly fascinating. "We wanted to know . . ."

"Are you trying to kill Adolf Hitler?" Gerta said. Her words tumbled out breathlessly. "Is that why the man came here to give you those papers? And what *are* those papers? And how do you know him? How do—"

Papa put up a hand. "Slow down, Gerta. And please, lower your voice."

She took a breath. "We deserve to know the truth, because if the Gestapo come to take you away, they'll take all of us away. Right, Maxi?"

She cocked her head and looked at him, imploring him to back her up. He glanced at Mutti, who was regarding her children with a curious expression.

His heart pounded. No way to unknow a secret . . .

"Right," he said at last. "We just want to know what's going on."

Papa took a long pull on his pipe and blew smoke into the air above the table.

"Karl," Mutti said.

"Ingrid," Papa said thoughtfully.

Max wondered what they were really saying to each other. Sometimes it seemed as if his parents had a private code, but instead of using nonsense that had to be deciphered, they were able to pack entire conversations in one or two words, often just by saying each other's names.

Suddenly, the mournful howl of Berlin's air-raid siren split the evening open like a wound. Max moved by instinct, the air-raid procedure drilled deep down into his brain at this point in the war. He jumped up from the table and threw open the kitchen window. Biting-cold air swirled into the house. He ran to open the front door and wedged a triangular piece of wood underneath it to prop it open. He did the same with the back door, and then rushed to open the rest of the windows.

Upstairs in his room, he paused to look out across Dahlem, over the peaked gables of neighboring villas, barely there in the darkness, to the distant Tiergarten, where the hulking monstrosity of the zoo flak tower sent searchlights slicing up through the night. Massive guns bristled at each corner of the cement fortress, and soon enough they would fill the sky with deafening flak bursts.

Gerta would already be down in the shelter, throwing the switches to turn off the electricity, gas, and water. Mutti would be gathering fresh food to supplement the rations they stored in the cellar. And Papa would do the final check to make sure the sandbags were in place and no light could leak out.

Max knew he should be hurrying down into the shelter, but he couldn't tear himself away from the window. His room had the best view in the house. If he lingered long enough, he would be able to see the first wave of British bombers break into Berlin's airspace.

"Max!" Mutti shouted from downstairs.

"Coming!" he shouted back.

And then he saw it: caught in a searchlight's beam, the green-and-black camouflaged underbelly of an Avro Lancaster. Behind it, dozens more British aircraft crept across the night sky, darkly gleaming birds in a formation so vast they seemed to cover the city's western suburbs like a canopy.

All at once, the flak guns atop the zoo tower opened up. Each cloudburst sent shock waves that Max felt in his stomach: *BOOM BOOM BOOM.*

The crackle of machine-gun fire came next, tracer bullets

arcing up to ping and spark against the steel wings and bellies of the Avro Lancasters.

Max stood transfixed. It felt as though he were watching a film, and yet at any moment the bombers could burst through the screen and destroy everything in their path.

There was a bright flash in the sky, and shattered pieces of fuselage and wings plummeted to earth in fiery comet-tail arcs. An unlucky bomber had taken a direct hit from an anti-aircraft shell. Max strained to see if the crew had managed to parachute out, but it was too dark and chaotic to tell.

Only when the first explosions sent billowing towers of flame across the city center did Max break free of the scene framed in his bedroom window and head downstairs to join the others in the basement shelter.

SEVEN

Before the war, the Hoffmanns' basement had been used for storing dry goods, wine, and things that weren't quite junk, but weren't urgently needed—old bicycles, boxes of newspapers, medical journals, reference books, tools, and model-building kits from when Papa was a boy. Max had always been a little bit frightened of the basement, with its damp chill and musty smell like that of a tomb, and the spider-webs that clung to his face as he moved about in the dark.

It hadn't helped that for the entire year of 1938, when Max was seven, Gerta had been sneaking scraps of food into the basement to feed the "cave troll" that she insisted lived down there.

As the last one into the shelter, Max shut the door behind him and pressed the rubber seal into place to fill the gaps between the door and its frame. This was to help protect the Hoffmanns from a poison gas attack, along with the four buglike gas masks hanging on hooks in the far corner of the shelter.

Thankfully, they'd never had to use them. But German official propaganda maintained that the British and their allies would not hesitate to send clouds of mustard gas hissing down to choke the population of Berlin.

Max descended the concrete steps to join Gerta and his parents in the wan flickering of the single kerosene lantern they used to illuminate the shelter.

Mutti was already wrapped in a quilt to ward off the chill, and Gerta handed Max his fluffy down jacket.

During the early months of the war, Papa had transformed the basement according to the *luftschutzwart*'s rules: the ceiling was strengthened with planed boards; narrow bunk beds and benches were built against two walls, while a third was lined with shelves that held provisions, emergency rations, folded blankets, towels, gloves, candles, matches, and two battery-powered torches. Half a dozen large buckets were filled with water at all times, while another three were filled with sand. In the center of the room was a table upon which sat the lantern and a deck of playing cards. The four rectangular windows set high into each wall were blocked from the outside with piles of sandbags.

As the Hoffmanns settled in, Gerta looked questioningly at Papa.

"You were saying?" she said.

The impact of the first wave of bombs sounded dull and muted underground, and the cellar barely shook—the raid tonight was concentrated far from Dahlem. Still, the flak fire was loud and startling.

"I don't believe I was saying anything," Papa said, taking the playing cards from their pack and idly shuffling them with his elegant hands.

"Karl," Mutti said. Her tone was different than it had been upstairs, and once again Max wondered how they managed to say so much by saying so little.

Papa set the cards down in a neat stack and fiddled with the lamp. The flame inside the glass burned brighter, sending jittery shadows into every corner of the basement.

"You know that we always try to be honest with you both," Papa said. "It is important for you to know that the Nazis are liars. We are not." He paused as a rapid-fire series of flak bursts shook the house. Dirt fell from the ceiling beams in a fine mist, speckling the table. Papa glared at the ceiling in distaste. No matter how often they cleaned the cellar, it was always covered in a thin layer of dust.

"All this"—he pointed at the ceiling, meaning the raids, the bombs, perhaps the war itself—"has forced you to grow up fast." He shook his head. "Much too fast," he said softly, almost as if he were talking only to himself. He paused for a moment to look at Max and Gerta in turn, and folded his hands in his lap before continuing. "Germany is going to lose this war."

Max's chest felt hot, and his body tingled at his father's words. The Nazis did not hesitate to execute civilians who uttered such treasonous things.

"Germany *should* lose this war," Mutti added. "Hitler has dragged us into madness. He doesn't care if all of Germany ends up like Hamburg."

Max remembered this past summer, when the Allies fire-bombed the city of Hamburg into oblivion. With their homes burned to the ground, refugees poured into Berlin, their only possessions the burnt rags they wore on their backs.

"The invasion of the Soviet Union was folly to begin with, and now Stalingrad is all but lost," Papa said. "And Germany's biggest ally in Europe—Italy—has surrendered to the Allies. The tide is turning, as many of us always knew it would. But even these recent defeats have not hastened the end like we'd hoped."

"Every day the Nazis remain in power," Mutti interjected, "is another day of shame for the German people."

"Yes," Papa agreed. "And so it is up to us to find the fastest route to peace, before Germany is wiped off the map and count-less more lives are lost in the camps and on the battlefields."

"For the sake of humanity—" Max said, echoing the words of the man who had died on the kitchen table.

"—the Führer must die," Gerta said, finishing his sentence.

Max knew Adolf Hitler as a strident voice on the radio, a voice that shouted and blustered from the speakers the Nazis placed on nearly every street corner in Berlin. He pictured Hitler as a figure on a podium at the head of a Nazi rally, whipping thousands of jackbooted soldiers and fanatically loyal civilians into a frenzy. When Hitler was in Berlin, he lived in the heavily guarded Reich Chancellery on Wilhelmstrasse, surrounded by his inner circle, guarded by elite SS troops. It wasn't like Hitler walked freely among the citizens of Berlin, went to the bakery and the cinema, took the trains to the office. How was somebody like Papa going to kill the most feared and powerful man in Germany—maybe in the entire world?

"They'll shoot you, Papa," Gerta said, voicing Max's thoughts. "The SS will shoot you before you can get anywhere near him."

"I don't plan to be anywhere near him," Papa said.

"Then how will you do it?" Max asked.

"It's complicated," Papa said, catching Mutti's eye.

"Karl," she said.

"Ingrid," he replied. "Do you think that's a good idea?"

Mutti narrowed her eyes slightly.

"Fine, then." Papa sighed. "Gerta. Max. We are not alone in this." He nodded once, as if convincing himself. "Tomorrow, you will meet Frau Becker."

EIGHT

The next morning, ash rained down from the sky.

A naval officer came to the Hoffmanns' door with a wet towel wrapped around his face, covering his mouth and nose. He lowered the towel briefly and explained that the wind had kicked up firestorms that were still burning in nearby Schmargendorf. School was canceled for the day.

The officer replaced the wet towel over his face and moved on to deliver the news to the Hoffmanns' neighbors. Papa shut the door.

"There will be burn victims," he said. "More than the hospitals can handle."

He strode purposefully into the small bathroom just off the living room and came out a moment later holding a dripping towel. Mutti fastened it around his face, and he went out into the gray, smoky morning.

Max spent much of the day staring out of his bedroom

window at the red haze that had settled over Berlin. The city glowed like embers in a fireplace—as if its molten core had been exposed, its fragile shell ripped away by the British bombs. He thought again of the refugees from Hamburg, skin blackened with soot, eyes staring off into the distance at horrors they would never forget.

Mutti and Papa blamed Hitler and the Nazis for all this suffering. But weren't the Allies partially to blame, too? After all, it was their incendiary bombs that had turned Hamburg into a fiery hellscape and reduced the whole city to ash. On the radio, the Nazi propaganda minister Joseph Goebbels called the bombing raids "terror attacks," and used them as proof that the Allies were monsters. But Max knew that the German air force—the Luftwaffe—had spent much of 1940 and 1941 bombing British cities. The campaign of German air attacks even had a name—the Blitz. And so back and forth it went, back and forth it would go, until . . . what? The great cities of Berlin and London were nothing but scorched black smudges on the landscape?

For a moment, he sank into deep despair. It was all so overwhelming, the machinery of war. And war seemed to have a mind of its own. It was as if people like Hitler had wound war up, charged its motor, and released it to wreak havoc across the world.

Would killing Hitler really put an end to all this, or would his assassination be one more spark added to the conflagration?

And who on earth was Frau Becker?

Questions swirled in Max's head as the smoke and ash whipped across the city. These questions would not be answered on this day, or during the night that followed. Papa did not come home. He managed to call to let his family know that he was fine, but he would have to stay the night at the hospital.

That night, mercifully, the air-raid sirens were silent, and Max actually managed to get some sleep.

The next day was Saturday. The air was free of ash and smoke, the sun came out, and Papa came home.

"I'm going to take a bath," he announced to Max and Gerta. "Then you two will do the same. Frau Becker does not take kindly to smelly guests."

NINE

Perleberger Strasse was lined with three-story row houses fronted by small, neatly kept lawns, stately facades, and large picture windows. As the Hoffmanns rounded the corner, Max saw that some of these windows had been blown out, but other than that, the street had escaped the recent raids unscathed. In front of several houses, scaffolding had been erected, and workmen were busy reinstalling glass in the window frames.

Pick up the pieces, sweep up, and move on.

Max pulled his scarf up to cover the lower half of his face. Despite the sunshine, the air was freezing, and there was a lingering acrid odor that stung his nose and mouth. To make matters worse, Papa had insisted that Max and Gerta wear their Sunday best, as if they were going to church services on Christmas. His wool vest itched, and his necktie felt like it was choking him. But he supposed it could be worse—he could have nothing but stockings to cover his legs, like his sister, who was wearing a dress the color of a robin's egg.

Despite being awake all night tending to burn victims, Papa was in high spirits.

"He's looking forward to the food," Mutti said. "You'll see."

Papa led them up the steps of a house near the end of the street. Max took in a few small, intriguing details—the wrought-iron railing that curled around itself in odd spirals, bricks the color of honey, and an ornate brass door knocker shaped like a gargoyle with its tongue sticking out.

Papa grabbed the gargoyle's face and slammed it against the heavy wooden door—two quick knocks in rapid succession, followed by two more at longer intervals.

A moment later, the door swung open. A middle-aged man in servant's livery scanned the four faces on his doorstep. Then he gave Papa and Mutti a shallow bow—just a nod of the head, really—and ushered them inside. The servant had bushy white eyebrows like a sea captain in an adventure tale. As he stepped into the front hall, Max noticed that where the man's left hand should be was an empty sleeve, pinned together at the end.

"French machine gun at the Somme," the servant said.

Max quickly looked away. The man had caught him staring!

"Chewed me up good," the man continued genially. "I was lucky an arm's all I lost."

"Sorry, Albert," Mutti said, shooting Max a pointed look. "He knows better than to stare."

"Ah, it's nothing, Ingrid," the man called Albert said. "Allow me to take your coats, and then come in by the fire. I'm getting cold just looking at you." As the Hoffmanns unwrapped scarves and unbuttoned coats for Albert to pile on his good arm, Max nudged Gerta. The front hall was lined with dark wood paneling and portraits of gentlemen from what looked like the last century, many of them wearing monocles and colorful military emblems and medals. There were ladies, too, in enormous billowing dresses. Gerta pointed at one young lady cradling a Labrador puppy as if it were a baby.

This Frau Becker had funny taste in art.

"The Beckers have been an aristocratic Prussian family for more than two centuries," Papa said as Albert retreated into a small cloakroom to hang coats and scarves on metal hangers. "These portraits are Frau Becker's ancestors."

Albert popped back out of the cloakroom and they followed him down the hall. Max began to hear voices—it sounded as if a lively party was already underway.

They came to a sumptuous red-velvet curtain. Albert moved it aside and beckoned for the Hoffmanns to cross the threshold into a large sitting room.

A fire crackled in a massive stone fireplace, immediately warming Max's bones. Seated on plush lounges and armchairs were five people—two of them about Papa and Mutti's age, two younger, and one much older.

This older one was a woman, and she was positively ancient. She perched on the edge of a wicker chair, one gnarled hand curled around the grip of a cane, the other holding a leather-bound book in her lap. Her face was etched with lines, and on her head was a round furry hat like Russian soldiers wore.

"Aha!" she said. Her astonishingly clear voice sliced through the chatter of the others in the room. "The guests of honor have arrived. Gerta and Max, I presume. Meet my new hat." She pointed to the furry cap on her head, which reminded Max of the pelt of a large rodent. "I am told it is called an *ushanka*. Princess Vasiliev was kind enough to spirit it away from the country estate in Königsberg. We need all the hats we can get right here in Berlin!"

"Frau Becker," said a raven-haired woman reclining on a lounge with a saucer and teacup balanced in her lap, "enough with the 'princess,' please." Her German was heavily accented. She turned to Max and Gerta. "Lovely to meet you. You may call me Marie."

Frau Becker shrugged. "I wanted them to be suitably impressed. It's not every day one meets a real princess."

Marie snorted. "These days I'm about as much a princess as General Vogel."

She lifted a stockinged foot and pointed her toes in the

direction of a large, big-bellied man in the spotless olive-green uniform of a high-ranking Wehrmacht officer, sporting a mustache that made him resemble a walrus. The Wehrmacht made up the bulk of Germany's fighting forces—the millions of ground troops that were currently fortifying the Atlantic coastline in the west and trudging across frigid Russia in the east.

"Karl, Ingrid, good to see you again," General Vogel said. "And it's nice to meet you," he said to Max and Gerta. "I've heard so much about you. I've got a daughter about your age— my Kat is nearly thirteen. She is the most marvelous—"

"Quiet, man, let them get some food!" Frau Becker said, waving her hand dismissively at General Vogel.

To Max's surprise, the general immediately stopped talking and sipped from a glass of wine.

"The duck pâté is delightful," said a young man seated to the left of the princess. He was thin and high-cheekboned, with a shock of blond hair combed to one side, smartly dressed in a fashionable gray suit adorned with a purple pocket square. His plate was heaped with food—bread and cheese, venison schnitzel, puff pastries. He set his plate down and approached the Hoffmanns.

"Max, Gerta," Mutti said, "this is Hans Meier, a medical student from Switzerland who visits us from time to time."

"Whenever I can, although the trains are becoming

positively abominable." Hans, too, spoke accented German. "I heard that it sometimes takes eight hours to get from the city center out to Potsdam." He shook hands with Papa and Mutti, then sat down cross-legged on the plush carpet in front of Max and Gerta. "It occurs to me that duck pâté might not be your favorite snack. In that case . . ."

He flashed his empty palms, then reached behind Max's ear with a quick, darting movement, as if he were grabbing a fish from a stream. When he pulled back, his hand was closed into a fist, which he slowly opened. In his palm sat two gold-foil-wrapped chocolate bonbons.

Max was speechless. He had not seen a piece of chocolate in Berlin since 1942.

"For me?" he asked, hesitating.

Hans gave him a look of mock reproach. "One for you, one for your sister, of course."

"Right," Max said. Slowly, he took the chocolate from Hans's palm, while Gerta did the same. He turned to Papa in disbelief. "Can we eat these right now?"

Papa chuckled. "Yes, Max. I don't see any reason to wait."

Papa and Mutti went to a small table against the far wall and began filling plates from a row of steaming serving trays. Max wondered how Frau Becker managed to host a Saturday salon as if there were no war at all. He knew there was a thriving black market that operated in Berlin—before her kitchen garden bloomed, Mutti sometimes bought fresh peas and carrots this way—and he supposed that as an aristocrat, Frau Becker had lots of money to buy goods outside of the ration system. But an old woman and a one-armed servant hobbling around the shadows of the Anhalter Station, furtively buying duck pâté and venison, seemed absurd to him.

As if summoned by Max's thoughts, Albert crossed the room with a bottle of wine and placed it into a silver ice bucket next to the table. Then he exited as swiftly as he'd arrived.

"Mmm," Gerta said, chewing her bonbon. "Amazing." She gave a little curtsy, which Max had never before seen her do. "Thank you, Herr Meier."

Max unwrapped his piece, enjoying the crinkle of the thin foil wrapper. Instead of popping the whole thing in his mouth, he began to nibble, savoring each sweet and slightly bitter bite.

"Switzerland," Hans said with a grin. "Come for the Alps, stay for the chocolates."

"I'll take an average German milk chocolate over the finest Swiss dark any day of the week," said the fifth stranger in the room. He was standing by the fire with his arms folded—an impeccably dressed gentleman, slightly older than Papa, with a pince-nez perched at the end of his nose.

Hans rolled his eyes and stood up. "Herr Trott is our

resident nationalist. He owns a tire factory. The war has made him very rich."

Herr Trott took a step forward into the lamplight, and Max saw the ugly scar that ran from above his left eye, down his nose, and across his right cheek to his jaw. "Listen to me, Meier," Herr Trott said, "I've been fighting the Nazis since you were in swaddling clothes."

Max finished his chocolate. He hoped the rich flavor would linger in his mouth for hours, and vowed not to eat or drink anything else at Frau Becker's that might wash it away. Chocolate brought him back to a time before the war, when Meyer's Candy Store was a solid building and not a ruined shell, and he could get chocolates from a huge jar for a pfennig. The idea that the city might one day run out of such a wonderful thing was beyond imagination. Everybody loved chocolate.

"Gentlemen, please," Frau Becker said. "We're all on the same side in here." She pointed the tip of her cane toward the front door. "The enemy is out there."

Hans winked at Max, then went back to his chair. Herr Trott glowered at the fireplace.

For a moment, no one spoke. And then the princess sat up with a jolt, spilling some of her tea into the rim of the saucer.

"Tiger's whiskers!" she blurted out. "An old zoologist friend of mine once told me that tiger's whiskers—chopped up fine and mixed with food—have been used to assassinate people throughout history. It's completely undetectable."

"Where are we going to get tiger's whiskers, Marie?" Mutti said. "It's nearly impossible to get an artichoke these days."

"If only the damned RAF hadn't bombed the zoo," the princess muttered.

Papa cleared his throat. "Perhaps it's time for more practical matters," he said. "Max, may I have your jacket?"

Max didn't understand, but he hated wearing the wool suit jacket, and now that they were in a warm, cozy room, he was beginning to sweat. So he was happy to oblige. He took off his jacket and handed it to Papa, who laid it flat across a small end table next to the sofa.

Then Papa took out a switchblade knife, flicked it open, and began carefully sawing into the lining of the jacket. Max's mouth dropped open. A moment later, his father produced the packet of papers the dead man had delivered.

No wonder his parents had insisted that he wear his Sunday best—Max's outfit was the hiding place!

TEN

Bring it here, Karl," Frau Becker said. It seemed to Max that her tone had become solemn. Then it struck him that the man who had died at the Hoffmanns' kitchen table was one of them—part of the group who met in this sitting room. Everyone here probably knew the man well.

Hans picked up a small collapsible serving tray and set it up like a table in front of Frau Becker. The old woman produced a pair of spectacles and put them on. Papa untied the twine that bound the bloodstained papers together and flattened the pages out carefully on the tray table. Everyone in the room, including Max and Gerta, gathered around the table, jostling for space so they could see.

Only General Vogel remained seated. "Good God, man!" He raised his voice at Papa. "You used your son as a courier! Why, if he had been stopped and searched . . . Well, I think we both know what would have happened!"

Max blinked. He supposed this was true, but it had not occurred to him to be angry at his father. *"Sippenhaft,"* Max said, gathering his courage to talk to the red-faced general. "The blood laws. It wouldn't matter whether the Gestapo found the papers on Papa or me. We would all be arrested." He looked from face to curious face. "Right?" Hans winked at him. Mutti looked pained.

"Yes, young man," Frau Becker said fiercely, with a glance toward General Vogel. "You provided us with the safest hiding place. The Gestapo aren't likely to search good German children for no reason. At least, not yet."

Max felt conflicted. He was glad that Frau Becker was pleased, but now the thought of a Gestapo agent searching him had wormed its way into his mind and would not fade away. Gestapo agents were not gentle or kind. They did not politely knock on doors; they pounded on them and screamed at whomever was inside to open up. They did not perform casual searches, but roughly patted people down in the street. He imagined the coarse hands of a towering agent ripping open his jacket, finding the hidden papers, grabbing him by the wrists, marching him toward the waiting green minna— one of the windowless trucks the Gestapo used to transport prisoners.

"You could have told us before we left the house," Gerta said to Papa. "You're supposed to be telling us the truth."

Papa looked chastened. "I thought it would be better if you didn't know. In the event we got stopped, I didn't want you to act nervous."

"But from now on," Mutti said, "no more secrets." She glanced at the others. "We are a team, and we need to act like one."

"My Kat knows nothing of this," General Vogel grumbled, "and that's the way it will remain."

"That is your choice, General," Papa said. "Not all of us have that luxury." He indicated the bloodstains on the papers. "Max and Gerta have already seen too much."

Frau Becker smoothed one of the papers—there were three, Max noted—and leaned forward to peer at it closely.

"Ah," she said. "The Wolfsschanze. Very good."

Max shot Gerta a questioning look. She shrugged. *The Wolf's Lair?* It sounded like something from a fantasy kingdom. The paper itself was no help—it was a printed map full of tiny squiggles for roads and boxes for what Max guessed were buildings.

General Vogel joined them at the little table. "The Wolf's Lair is Hitler's headquarters in the east," he explained to Max and Gerta, "in what used to be Poland."

Suddenly, Herr Trott jabbed a finger into one of the boxes on the map, startling Max. Out of everybody in the sitting room, Herr Trott was the most intimidating—the only one of

Frau Becker's guests who actually scared him. "This is the reinforced bunker, here," Herr Trott said. "This is where he'll meet with Himmler and Göring."

When Herr Trott named Hitler's trusted advisors, Max's thoughts churned. Was Frau Becker's group planning to assassinate the entire Nazi high command?

"Mmm," Frau Becker said, lost in thought. "Perhaps, perhaps."

She shuffled to the next page and smoothed it out. "The Kehlsteinhaus," she muttered. "I'm not so sure about this."

"The Eagle's Nest," Max said. He'd heard of this place. It was the most famous of Hitler's headquarters outside of Berlin, an impregnable fortress perched on top of a mountain.

"Correct," Frau Becker said. "Give this boy a cookie." When nobody moved, she turned to Marie. "Go on, Princess."

Marie shrugged. "I was getting one for myself anyway."

"The Eagle's Nest is quite a remote possibility," Papa said. "I like our chances best at the Führerbunker. If you'll kindly go to the next page."

Frau Becker set the Eagle's Nest map aside and smoothed out the third and final piece of paper.

"It's right here in Berlin, for starters," Papa continued. "Accessible by the largest number of personnel."

"Construction isn't finished," General Vogel pointed out.

"They're still building the new wing." He indicated some lines on the map. "There will be living quarters here."

"Even so, it is where Hitler waits out the air raids," Papa said. "We know when he will be there."

"He doesn't tend to hold big military conferences in the Führerbunker," General Vogel said.

"Exactly right," Herr Trott said. "If we focus on the Wolf's Lair, we can get all the bastards in one place."

"*Pssst!*" Max and Gerta turned at the sound. Princess Marie was behind them, holding up two sugar cookies. She was also munching one herself.

Eagerly, they took the cookies from the princess. Max forgot all about his earlier vow to let the flavor of the chocolate linger, and in two big bites the cookie was gone and he was wiping crumbs from the corner of his mouth.

"I will have to think about this," Frau Becker said, neatly folding the papers back into a small square. "And then I will make a recommendation. We will put it to a vote before we approach our counterparts."

Max glanced at Gerta. *Counterparts?* Who else was involved in this plot?

"In the meantime," Frau Becker continued, gently thwacking Max on the side of the arm with her cane, "I have a job for you." She did the same to Gerta. "And you."

"What kind of a job?" Gerta said, eyes wide with excitement.

"Frau Becker," Mutti said, "we agreed that Max and Gerta should not be kept in the dark after what they saw, but we said nothing about them becoming active members of the resistance. They should know the truth, of course, but there's no reason to expose them to any further danger."

"And what, precisely, do you call sewing maps of the Führer's headquarters inside the boy's jacket?" Frau Becker asked.

"A one-time, unavoidable event," Mutti said.

The old woman shook her head. "Every day, more of our Jewish neighbors—Berliners, just like us!—are hunted down like dogs by the Nazis and shipped to the death camps."

At the sound of *death camps*, Max's legs turned to jelly. He so rarely heard them called that. Most other grown-ups, like his teacher and the *blockwart*, called them *relocation centers*.

"And yet we hide our heads in the sand," Frau Becker said.

Aha! Max thought. *That's where Mutti got the expression.*

"We are all doing what we can, Frau Becker," the princess said.

"It's not enough," the old woman replied. "It's never enough." She placed a hand on the packet of maps. "But I am afraid this operation will take time to plan. We must be very careful not to rush out of our desire to have it done quickly. It must be done right—we may only get one chance."

Max looked from the princess to Herr Trott to Hans, from General Vogel to his parents. Who among them would be the one to walk up to Adolf Hitler and kill him? Or was the assassin one of the mysterious counterparts of which Frau Becker had spoken?

"In the meantime," Frau Becker continued, "we shall step up our efforts here in Berlin."

"What can we do?" Gerta asked eagerly.

"There are Jews hiding right here in the city, under the noses of the Gestapo," Hans said. "But without ration cards, it is difficult for them to survive. They must rely on the scraps from friendly tables. And for those who wish to escape Germany entirely, it is nearly impossible to move about the streets without the proper papers. So, either way, they need forged identification documents. That is where we come in."

"I print the pages in the basement of my factory," Herr Trott said. "There's so much old equipment and machinery down there, it would take the Gestapo a hundred years to figure out there's a working printing press shoved into a dark corner."

"I work in the Foreign Office," the princess said, "on magazine layouts. I take care of the finishing touches—the photographs and such."

"We have become rather skilled at creating the forgeries themselves," Frau Becker explained. "What continues to vex us is the last step—getting the papers into the hands of the people who need them. We are rather . . . recognizable." She smiled. "That, my friends, is where *you* come in."

"We'll do it!" Gerta said.

"Frau Becker," Papa said, "can we speak privately about this?"

"No," Mutti said. She took a deep breath and let it out. "I promised no more secrets. They can make up their own minds."

"Er," Max said, "to do *what*, exactly?"

Hans reached behind Max's ear. When he opened his fist, there was a piece of yellow chalk in his palm. "You'll need this, my friend."

ELEVEN

November slid icily into December. The days turned cold, the nights frigid. One night, during the first week of the month, bombers raiding Berlin were scattered by crosswinds to the southern districts of the city. The next morning, a light snow fell, mingling with ash to coat the streets in a drab gray slush, thin as the gruel that passed for soup in the city's remaining restaurants.

Along the wide Altensteinstrasse at the eastern edge of Dahlem, near the botanical garden, Max and Gerta walked on opposite sides of the street. Bundled in heavy coats, hats, and scarves, they were indistinguishable from the other pedestrians hurrying home in the dying light of a winter dusk, turning their collars up against the chill.

When Max came to the second bombed-out apartment block along the route laid out by the Becker Circle, stark and sullen against the unfriendly sky, he slowed down to read the ruins.

Ever since the first RAF raids in 1940, Berliners had been scrawling messages in chalk on the ruins of buildings, letting friends and loved ones know they survived the bombing.

Josef, we are unhurt, find us in the university shelter,
    love T
My darling Gaby, I saved the cat
Papa, I am staying with Loremarie, love Luzie

Max glanced furtively across the street. Gerta ducked beneath the front stoop of an undamaged row house, into the little shelter under the stairs for garbage cans and refuse.

He shot a quick look over his shoulder and waited for a man in a trench coat to pass by, averting his eyes. Gestapo agents weren't like the SS, with their starched uniforms and thudding footsteps. They often worked undercover, wearing civilian clothes, blending in. Max wouldn't know if he'd been caught until it was too late.

Directly across from where Gerta had ducked beneath the stairs, Max chose a stack of bricks with metal rebar jutting out at the top, high above his head. It was unlikely to collapse in the next day or so. Quickly, he removed the glove on his right hand and fished the chalk out of his pocket. Careful not to break the chalk with his freezing fingers, he wrote a message on the bricks according to the code for the day.

Dear Jürgen, don't worry about me, I've gone to Potsdam

Satisfied, Max stuck the chalk back in his pocket and moved on down the street. He risked one quick look behind him at the ruins, and when he turned his head back, he bumped into a man hurrying in the opposite direction.

Thrown off balance, Max spun halfway around as the man strode away down the sidewalk without so much as an "excuse me," trench coat flapping in his wake. Max stared after the man for as long as he dared. Was it the same person he'd seen a moment ago, heading in the other direction, just before he'd chalked the ruins?

Maybe the man suddenly realized he'd forgotten something important at home, and had to turn around and rush back.

Or maybe he'd seen Max acting suspiciously and decided to get a closer look.

That was the strange paradox of Berliners—they hid their heads in the sand when it came to the Gestapo rounding up Jews and political agitators, but they were only too happy to inform on their neighbors about the slightest offenses. Papa called it "selective awareness." Whatever it was called, it meant that the Gestapo weren't Max and Gerta's only worry—they had to keep calm and act normal around *everyone.*

He watched the man in the trench coat disappear around a bend in the Altensteinstrasse. Then he glanced across the street, just as Gerta emerged from beneath the front stoop of the row house. They walked briskly toward the northwest corner of the botanical garden. He was breathing as if he'd just run a race, exhaling white puffs into the air.

This will get easier, he told himself. He caught the eye of a tall, stylish woman, who peered at him from beneath a smart, tilted hat. As he looked away, he thought, *Should I have held eye contact?* It was hard to remember what acting normal was supposed to look and feel like. He felt totally exposed, as if he were wearing a sign that said SPY. He began to concentrate on the way he was walking, trying to keep his stride casual, but that only made things worse. It was difficult to walk normally when you were telling yourself: *Walk normally.*

At the corner of the botanical garden, where the high stone gave way to a wrought-iron gate, he finally crossed paths with Gerta. She gave him a quick nod—*it's done*—and walked past him, skirting the edge of the garden to the east, while he moved along the street to the south.

Sometime in the next few hours, one of the Becker Circle's contacts in the Jewish underground would move quickly down the Altensteinstrasse, discover Max's coded signal, cross the street to the stoop directly across from his chalk scrawl, and find the forged identification papers that Gerta had hidden behind a garbage can.

Max and Gerta would never see this person or contact him or her directly. This kind of separation was how the resistance operated. That way, if operatives got picked up by the Gestapo and broke under torture, they could only give up limited information about the anti-Nazi resistance, its members, and its activities.

As he walked toward the station where he would catch a train home, Max once again removed his glove and slipped his hand into the pocket of his jacket. His fingers brushed against the foil of the last piece of chocolate Hans had given him, which he'd managed to save as a reward for a successful "dead drop"—the name Papa gave to Max and Gerta's job.

He thought about waiting until he got home. Then he unwrapped the foil and popped the chocolate into his mouth. All around him, the snow fell heavier. Eventually, it triumphed over the ash, and, for a little while at least, Berlin sparkled.

TWELVE

Dahlem's *blockwart*, Franz Siewert, glanced out the window of his cramped office. The snow had picked up, and the blast of winter brought with it memories of backbreaking labor. As a child, he had rushed outside with his shovel during snowstorms, pounding on doors, offering to clear out walkways and steps for a few marks.

Herr Siewert had always been ambitious. And now, with the war in full swing, the opportunities for advancement were greater than ever. All of his failures of the 1930s—his doomed landscaping business, the bratwurst stand in the Tiergarten that had been muscled out by the competition—would be wiped away once he joined the Schutzstaffel.

The SS.

What had begun as Hitler's personal bodyguard had transformed, under the brilliant leadership of Heinrich Himmler, into the army-within-the-army, responsible for enforcing Nazi policy throughout the Reich.

In the SS, there was no limit to how high a crafty, industrious man like Siewert might rise.

He lit the chewed-up remnants of a cigar, took a deep drag, and let the smoke curl lazily about the office. He pictured himself among the perfect ranks of the SS, marching in gorgeous, fearsome symmetry down Unter den Linden. He closed his eyes and imagined the crowd lining the avenue, the awestruck admiration in the faces of all those watching the parade.

There was his polished silver lightning bolt emblem glinting in the light from the great torches . . .

A knock on his office door shook him from his reverie.

"Come in!"

His secretary entered, set a folder carefully on his desk, and quickly retreated, closing the door behind her. She knew better than to make conversation. Siewert was a busy man and detested interruptions. It was this level of deep focus that would earn him a place at Himmler's side. And once the war was won . . . who knew? A cabinet ministry, perhaps, strolling the promenades of the spectacular buildings of Germania—the expanded, supersized Berlin, transformed into the glorious capital of the thousand-year Reich.

He opened the folder to find a memo on the Gestapo's

official letterhead, addressed to Dahlem's *blockwart*. It was an intelligence report gathered by a Gestapo spy planted inside one of the anti-Nazi resistance organizations operating right here in Berlin.

At first, Siewert merely scanned the report, idly enjoying the last puffs of his cigar. Then, suddenly, it captured his attention. He stabbed out the cigar in his ashtray and leaned forward, reading the report over again, savoring the words.

This resistance group was forging identity documents for Jews in hiding, so they could apply for ration cards, travel freely throughout Germany, and perhaps even cross the border if they were lucky.

Since 1942, the Nazis had decreed that all Jews living in Berlin had to wear a yellow star on their clothing. This made it possible to deny them service at shops where pure-blooded Aryans bought food and clothes, to force them to commute on special train cars, and to root them out of important jobs in order to keep government and university positions racially pure.

Siewert approved of these measures. Before the yellow stars, it could sometimes be difficult to tell which of his fellow Berliners were Jewish. He had unwittingly associated with them for years, shopping at Jewish-owned stores and even hoisting steins with them in the beer halls after a hard day's work.

The Nazis had made it much easier for Siewert to tell who it was right and proper for him to be associating with. And it was getting easier all the time—now there were far fewer Jews in the city than there had been at the start of the war. With all the territory the Third Reich was capturing, there was plenty of room to relocate the Jews to cities and camps in the east. Let them have Poland and Hungary, he thought. Leave Berlin to citizens like Franz Siewert—people with good blood.

He shoved the paper back into the folder and slammed it shut, bringing his palm down hard on the desk.

The notion of Jews once again hiding in plain sight, with forged papers that declared them to be part of Siewert's own race, drove him up and out of his chair. He paced the tiny office with his hands behind his back, like he had practiced many times before, imitating an SS interrogator prowling the interview room, savoring the moment while the prisoner squirmed and begged.

In this daydream, Siewert wore his freshly starched SS uniform with pride. People knew to get out of his way as he marched down the street, riding crop at his side, polished boots crushing anything in his path. After all, he was SS-Oberführer Siewert, the man who had smashed the most secretive and clever resistance group in all of Berlin. He had caught the plotters red-handed, along with the Jewish weasels who refused to wear the yellow star. For this, Heinrich

Himmler himself had plucked Franz Siewert from obscurity, promoting him from lowly *blockwart* to the top ranks of the SS.

Siewert went to the small round mirror on the wall. He fixed his spectacles, smoothed his thinning hair to one side, and removed a small fleck of tobacco stuck to the corner of his lip. He threw his shoulders back, puffed out his chest, and straightened his posture.

The Gestapo report had noted that the couriers working for the forgers were a pair of children who used coded messages in chalk as signals. These people thought they were so clever! Well, they underestimated just how vigilant a man like Herr Siewert could be.

In the mirror, he gave a German salute so crisp that he nearly dislocated his shoulder.

"Heil Hitler!"

THIRTEEN

By the time Max got home, dusk was creeping across the city, and the snow was up to his ankles. Despite wearing his scarf like a mask, his face was numb. He had grown more and more paranoid as he approached the train station and doubled back several times, walking in crazy loops around Dahlem to make sure the man in the trench coat wasn't following him home.

Mutti, Papa, and Gerta all jumped up from the living room sofa as soon as he burst through the door.

Mutti rushed to embrace him. "My God, Maxi, you're a block of ice! We were worried sick about you! Gerta has been back for an hour!"

Papa turned to Gerta. "Run a hot bath."

Gerta looked puzzled. "It's Thursday, Papa." To conserve water, baths were only allowed on weekends.

"Yes, but your brother needs thawing. Quickly now!"

Gerta rushed upstairs.

Mutti unwound the scarf from Max's face and pulled off his gloves. She cupped her hands around her mouth and breathed hot air on his hands.

How strange, thought Max, to be doing a dead drop on his own—the most grown-up thing he'd ever done—only to come home to his mother fussing over him.

"I'm fine," he said, gently pushing her hands away. He hung his hat on a peg and wormed his way out of his overcoat.

"I knew this was a bad idea," Mutti said.

"You were supposed to come straight home afterward," Papa said. "What kept you?"

Max hesitated. If he told his parents about the man in the trench coat, they might not let him go out on the next drop. Part of him thought that would be okay—his heart was still hammering in his chest, and he had never been so anxious in his life. But another part of him wanted desperately to show Frau Becker and the others—not to mention Gerta—that he was brave enough to resist the Nazis.

He remembered Mutti's words—*no more secrets*—and decided to tell the truth.

"I wasn't sure if somebody was watching me or not. I had to double back a few times to lose the tail. I didn't want to lead him back here, just in case."

Max had learned how to lose a tail from listening to *Hornet and Wasp*, but he left that part out.

The next thing he knew, Mutti and Papa were sitting him down on the sofa. Papa looked as serious as Max had ever seen. Mutti's eyes were wide as they looked into Max's.

"What did this man look like?" Papa said.

"Tall," Max said. "And he was wearing a long gray trench coat."

"What made him different than other people on the street?" Mutti said.

Max considered this for a moment. "I thought I saw him twice—once going one way, then again a minute later going the other way."

"You *thought* you saw him twice," Mutti said, "or you *did* see him?"

Max closed his eyes. He had only briefly glanced at the man, and between the falling snow and the brim of the man's hat, the face in Max's memory was nothing more than a pale smudge. He pictured the trench coat flapping in the man's wake as he hurried down the street, and then again in the opposite direction after Max bumped into him. It was frustrating, but there was nothing at all distinctive about the coat or the hat. It could have been the same person. It could just as easily have been two different people.

"I don't know," Max admitted.

Mutti threw up her hands. "This is foolish, Karl. Blood laws or no blood laws, this is too great a risk."

Papa patted Max's knee. "You did the right thing, Maxi. Better safe than sorry." Max looked down at his thick, fuzzy socks. If he did the right thing, why did it suddenly feel like he'd screwed up?

The simple fact was, Gerta was cut out for this kind of work. He wasn't.

There was a reason she handled the top-secret documents and Max handled the piece of chalk.

Gerta came bounding down the stairs, drying her hands on a flannel. "Bath's ready, icicle brother." She stopped in her tracks, reading the mood of the room. "What's going on? Who died?"

"You mother believes this courier work is too dangerous." Papa glanced at Max. "And I'm inclined to agree with her. Perhaps we were too hasty in letting Frau Becker involve you so heavily."

Gerta put her hands on her hips and glared at Max. "What on earth did you tell them?" She looked at Mutti. "It went perfectly fine! Don't listen to Max. He was afraid of the cave troll in the basement up until last year."

Papa frowned. "What cave troll?"

"Exactly," Gerta said.

"I'm sorry," Mutti said. "I'm just not comfortable with this. You got away clean this time; there's no need to push your luck any further."

"But Frau Becker—" Gerta protested.

"Will have to find another pair of couriers," Mutti said. "Now, Max, go take your bath before the water gets cold."

Max trudged up the stairs. Gerta's eyes burned into his back.

In the bathroom, he shut the door, undressed, sank into the warm water, and closed his eyes. He should have just kept his mouth shut, he thought. That was probably a good rule for a spy to take to heart.

FOURTEEN

Later that night, Max knocked on Gerta's bedroom door.

"Go away!" came the voice from inside.

"Come on," Max said. "I need to talk to you."

"Not interested!"

Max opened the door anyway. His sister was sitting on her bed, flipping listlessly through one of the American movie magazines her school friends traded among themselves. Max knew the magazine would be several months old, but it wasn't like anybody in Berlin could actually see American films, anyway. So it didn't really matter.

"You got a problem with your ears?" she said without looking up from the magazine.

Max shut the door behind him. "Gerta, I'm sorry, okay?"

She tossed the magazine aside and lay back to stare at the ceiling. "We finally got our chance to help fight the Nazis—to do something that actually makes a difference—and you got us kicked off the job after one day."

"All I did was tell Mutti and Papa the truth. I thought I saw—"

"You didn't see anything! Your mind was playing tricks."

"Maybe you're right, but this is serious, Gerta! I couldn't just lead him back to our house!"

"Shhh!" Gerta said, sitting up.

Max lowered his voice. "I was scared, okay? I was really scared."

Gerta took a deep breath and let it out. "I know. I'm not mad at you for that, Maxi. I was just happy to be doing *something*."

"So was I," Max said. He hesitated. He knew that he could change both of their lives with what he was about to say. He sat down on the bed and lowered his voice even further. "That's why I think we should go back."

Gerta frowned. "To Altensteinstrasse?"

"To Frau Becker's house," Max said. "Just us, I mean. Without telling Mutti and Papa."

Gerta's eyes flashed with excitement. "You think she'll give us another dead drop to do?"

Max shrugged. "Only one way to find out."

"We can go after school tomorrow," Gerta said. "Mutti will

be out at the market and Papa will be at the hospital. They'll never know if we're not home on time."

"Okay," Max said. "Then let's do it." He turned to leave.

"Max?" Gerta said. "One more thing. Out there on the street? I was scared, too."

FIFTEEN

Max reached up, grabbed the brass gargoyle's pointy nose, and slammed the knocker against Frau Becker's door in the same way he'd seen Papa do: two quick raps, then two at longer intervals.

A moment later, the door swung open and Albert greeted them.

"Hoffmanns!" He peered beyond Max and Gerta. "Well, half of you, anyway." He stepped aside and beckoned for them to come in.

"Is Frau Becker here?" Gerta asked as they stepped into the front hall.

"I should say so!" Albert exclaimed as he collected their coats. "Why, she hasn't set foot outside this house since the war started. Says she doesn't want to see her beloved Berlin until the last Nazi flag is lowered. I keep telling her, you might want to take a look-see sooner rather than later, because at this rate, there won't be much Berlin left when it's all over. But once that woman sets her mind to something . . ." He shook his head and disappeared into the cloakroom.

Max and Gerta stood among the portraits in silence until Albert returned a moment later to lead them through the red-velvet curtain and into the sitting room. Frau Becker was in her wicker chair, using a magnifying glass to read from a massive leather-bound book.

Albert cleared his throat, and she looked up.

"Ah," she said, as if she'd been expecting them all along. "There you are. Just in time for afternoon tea." She closed the book with a *thud* and waved away a cloud of dust that puffed up to wreathe her head. "Albert, do we have any of that wonderful baumkuchen left?"

"I believe we do."

"Three slices, then, please."

"Right away." Albert disappeared behind the curtain.

"Frau Becker, we don't have time to sit and have a snack," Gerta said. Max elbowed her in the arm. They could at least bring the cake with them!

"Nonsense," Frau Becker said. "Your father's shift at the hospital won't end until after ten, and I'm afraid your mother will be in for some long lines at the shops today. I hear they've all but run out of potatoes."

Max blinked. According to Albert, Frau Becker never left

her house—he doubted very much if she ever left her armchair—and yet she seemed to know everything that went on in Berlin.

"Please," she said, gesturing grandly toward the sofa. Max and Gerta sat down. Frau Becker hefted the enormous book with a grunt and set it on the table at her side. The title was embossed with gold leaf: *The Napoleonic Wars.*

"Your little errand was a smashing success," Frau Becker said. "Because of you two, a family that had been hidden away in an attic can move about more freely, and use ration cards instead of relying on the leftovers from their host's table."

"That's actually what we came to talk to you about," Max said.

"Your parents are squeamish about your new job," Frau Becker said. "They think the danger is too great."

Max's mouth dropped open. Was Frau Becker reading their minds? His eyes scanned the sitting room, searching for a crystal ball or some other evidence of sorcery. It didn't seem too far-fetched that an old aristocratic family might have dabbled in witchcraft . . .

"Here you go," Albert said, setting up a tray table. He was balancing three small plates on his arm, and one by one he transferred them to the table. It wasn't until he began pouring tea from a white ceramic pot that Max noticed with a start that Albert's appearance had changed dramatically.

"You have two arms!" he blurted out. This afternoon was getting stranger and stranger.

Albert chuckled. "That I do, my friend. Both in good working order."

Max studied the servant's face. There was something different about that, too—he sported a thin mustache, the lines in his forehead were deeper, and his cheeks seemed fuller, giving the impression of an older, heavier man.

"I rely on Albert for many different errands, requiring many different skills," Frau Becker explained. "It is safer for him, and for me, if the authorities don't often see the same man in the same places."

"What about the French machine gun," Gerta said, "at the Somme?"

"Must've just missed me," Albert said.

He winked at Max and left the room, moving with a slight limp that Max was certain he had not been afflicted with a moment ago.

Max felt like he was dreaming. Events he could only partially understand were swirling feverishly around him, and every time he grasped at something solid, it slithered out of his hands. Everything in Frau Becker's house—the velvet curtain, the portraits in the hall, the plush carpet, the slices of cake, Frau Becker herself—seemed to belong to a very mysterious and grown-up place.

More than ever, he wanted to be a part of something that transported him away from the drudgery of the raids, the meager rations, the air-raid shelter. How strange that escaping the eternal sameness of the war meant playing an even greater part in it.

"We came to ask you for another job," Max said.

Frau Becker peered at him through narrowed eyes. "All right. Here's a job for you. Can you find my hat? The one the princess kindly gave to me? I seem to have misplaced it."

"Frau Becker—we want to do another dead drop," Gerta said.

"Oh, I know what you mean." Frau Becker waved her hand dismissively. "I'm not entirely without my wits, girl." She sighed. "Sneaking around under the noses of the Gestapo is hard enough—now you want to pull the wool over your parents' eyes, too? They aren't fools, you know."

"They won't find out," Gerta insisted. Max didn't know how his sister could be so confident—there were a million ways for this to go wrong. But he kept his mouth shut.

"See that they don't," Frau Becker said. "The notion of Ingrid Hoffmann on my bad side does give me a slight pause."

"But—" Gerta protested.

Frau Becker held up a hand. "I said *slight.* The resistance needs you. Albert will give you a fresh packet of documents on your way out. The drop will be along the Messelstrasse at the southern edge of Messelpark, tomorrow night. Is that satisfactory?"

Max looked at his sister. His mouth was dry. Tomorrow night was much sooner than he'd anticipated! A new job had seemed like a distant proposition, something he could worry about in a week or two.

"Perfect," Gerta said.

"Fabulous," Frau Becker said. "Now eat your cake."

SIXTEEN

When Max and Gerta crept out of their beds just before midnight, they could tell right away that their father was sound asleep—his snoring sounded like a jet engine. Their mother was the problem—she could be sleeping contentedly at her husband's side, or reading quietly by the bedside lamp, kept awake by his ungodly snoring. Their parents kept their bedroom door closed, so there was no way to sneak a peek.

Max hoped that Mutti wasn't feeling restless. Sometimes, if Papa's snoring drove her to the brink of madness, she would go downstairs to read in the living room. Many times, Max had awakened in the middle of the night and gone quietly down to the kitchen for a glass of water, only to find his mother dozing with a book open in her lap and the blue-tinted lamp casting its eerie glow.

Tonight, thankfully, the house was dark and Mutti was nowhere to be seen.

Wordlessly, Max followed Gerta across the living room. They walked on stocking feet to mute their footsteps, only putting on their heavy boots when they reached the front door. Max patted the pocket of his overcoat to make sure he had the piece of chalk. In his head, he repeated the coded phrase to himself: *Karsten, I am well and staying with Belinda.*

Gerta put her hand on the doorknob. At the same time, a floorboard creaked, and she froze. Max noticed that the snoring had ceased. Papa was awake! His heart pounding, he stood perfectly still at his sister's side, listening. A moment later, the toilet flushed. There was more creaking, and then the squeaks of the mattress springs as Papa settled back into bed. Almost immediately, the snoring resumed.

Carefully, Gerta opened the front door. Max was struck by the absurd fear that the frigid blast of cold air would find its way upstairs and wake his parents. But there was no going back now. He followed Gerta out to the front stoop, and then watched with his heart in his throat as she shut the door as quietly as she could.

Outside, Dahlem was silent and still. A thin, wintry drizzle hung in the air—more icy mist than snowfall. In the sky above the city, ice crystals sparkled in the searchlights that brushed the undersides of the clouds. A few windows in their neighborhood leaked dim blue light, but the streets themselves were dark, the sidewalks empty. Streetlamps had not been lit for years, since the blackout rules began. A few blocks from home, they finally risked a whispered conversation.

"You sure you know the way?" Max said.

"For the hundredth time, yes," Gerta hissed. She was a much better navigator than he was. Messelpark wasn't far from where they lived—about a twenty-minute walk—but Max lost his bearings easily in the pitch-black night. He couldn't even see the street signs.

Silently, he calculated how long they would be gone. Twenty minutes out, twenty minutes back, plus a few minutes to find a good spot to chalk the coded message and hide the documents so that the Jewish underground could pick them up. If it all went well, they would only be missing from their beds for forty-five minutes. What were the chances that Mutti would get up and check on them in that narrow window of time?

"If they notice we're gone, do you think they'll call the police?" Max said.

They turned a corner and walked briskly up the street where they had helped the *ostarbeiters* clear the rubble from the raid in late November, back when Herr Siewert had invited him to join the Hitler Youth. Max remembered the telephone, hopelessly buried and ringing endlessly, as someone frantically tried to reach a relative or friend who would never answer.

"I don't know," Gerta said. "Don't think about it. Focus on what we're doing."

But Max couldn't help it. Seemingly out of his control, his thoughts bloomed into paranoia. Explaining to Mutti and Papa what they were doing sneaking around in the middle of the night was one thing, but explaining it to the police was quite another. There were plenty of policemen who would not hesitate to report anything suspicious to the Gestapo.

They took a sharp left and plunged suddenly into an even deeper darkness. It was as if the lid of the night had come down fully, blotting out the searchlights and the sky.

Max's breath caught in his throat. He felt like he was walking through a void.

"It's just the netting," Gerta said. "Relax."

Max let out his breath. To confuse RAF bombers, Berlin's air defense teams had strung camouflage netting along various streets. That way, the layout of the city would not correspond to the way it looked on maps, confusing pilots searching for specific targets from the air.

Max had no idea if it worked or not. With or without netting, planes came, bombs fell, houses crumbled, people died.

He reached out and held his sister's arm. Together, they moved through the darkness.

SEVENTEEN

Franz Siewert was freezing. The problem was his hands—his fingers were always numb, even inside their woolen mittens. He stuck them deeper into the pockets of his overcoat as he leaned against a sturdy oak at the edge of Messelpark.

The very day he received the Gestapo intelligence report about the resistance group, Siewert had put together a small vigilante squad of eight trusted friends from the beer hall—loyal Nazis, all of them. He could never hope to monitor all of Dahlem on his own, but with a team at his disposal, they could cover more ground and keep their eyes peeled for subversive activity. Even if one of his associates caught the couriers, Siewert could still take most of the credit. After all, he was the leader.

Then, earlier today, he received another memo on Gestapo letterhead. An urgent situation had developed: Another document drop was in the works—and it was happening tonight, near Messelpark.

Siewert had sent his associates fanning out across Dahlem, while he assigned himself the area of the drop. He was going to apprehend the criminals single-handedly and deliver them to the Gestapo personally. It wouldn't be long before Heinrich Himmler knew the name Franz Siewert.

He rolled the wet, unlit cigar from one side of his mouth to the other, keeping an eye on the buildings across from the park, several of which had been hit in a bombing raid last week. At the same time, his thoughts drifted toward the warm bath that awaited him at the end of the night. As *blockwart* he was exempt from the weekends-only bath rule.

Movement across the street caught his eye. Just another pedestrian hurrying home after a late-night shift, probably. Even at this quiet hour, in this frigid weather, scattered citizens roamed the streets. It sometimes amazed him that everyone hadn't already packed up and left Berlin a ghost town. There had been evacuations, especially of women and children, but an astonishing number of Berliners chose to stay and endure the war in the heart of the Reich. If, heaven forbid, the Soviets or the Americans ever reached the city, Berliners would fight them to the last man. Siewert swelled with pride at the glory of it all: Germans digging in and defending their homeland to the death.

Siewert brought his attention back to the matter at hand. There was something odd about the figure across the street. It seemed, suddenly, to split into two. He rubbed his eyes—surely the night was playing tricks on him. But then the second figure darted across Messelstrasse—a dark coat, the white of an eye—heading straight for him! Quietly, he slid behind the tree and observed. The figure halted about twenty paces from his hiding place, at the edge of the park where the lawn met the sidewalk. Siewert's heart began to pound. Oh, yes. This was good. This was some kind of subversive activity. Upstanding, law-abiding Germans didn't skulk in the shadows of Messelpark after midnight.

The figure was very short—a child, perhaps. Siewert watched as they knelt down in the grass and began to dig. How curious. He stepped out from behind the tree. His target seemed wholly absorbed and did not look up.

Siewert put his hand on the baton that dangled from a loop in his belt.

This was going to be fun.

EIGHTEEN

Max had just finished chalking the ruins when he heard his sister scream—an abrupt shriek that sent his heart up into his throat. Across the street, the edge of the park was lost in a sea of blackness. All he could do was dart off in the direction of her voice. It was hard enough to see at night in a blacked-out city, but the park, like the street beneath the camouflage netting, was a sightless void. He might as well be blindfolded. He stumbled when he hit the sidewalk on the other side and barely kept himself from tumbling.

"*Gerta!*" he whispered as loudly as he dared.

A man's gruff voice answered, startlingly close: "I've been waiting for you!"

Max thought he recognized the voice, but he had no time to think. He groped blindly. It wasn't until he was practically on top of them that the two figures materialized out of the darkness: a big man holding a girl by the arm while she flailed and kicked.

Franz Siewert and Gerta Hoffmann.

Without hesitating, Max launched himself between the *blockwart* and his sister. Siewert cried out in surprise. A crushing blow landed across Max's left shoulder. He hit the ground hard, thankful for his heavy coat. At the same time, Gerta twisted out of the man's grip and delivered a vicious kick to his left shin. Siewert howled in pain.

"Come on, Max!" she yelled. He scrambled to his feet. His shoulder throbbed. Siewert raised the baton to deliver another blow. Max barely had time to get a forearm up to block his face—

And then the air-raid siren began to wail, splitting the quiet night.

Siewert paused, just long enough for Max to jump out of the way as the baton came whistling past his face.

"This way!" Gerta yelled, and together they ran northwest along Messelpark, boots pounding down the cobblestones. Behind them, Max heard Siewert wheezing and puffing as he struggled to keep up.

"Stop them!" Siewert yelled. "By order of the Dahlem *blockwart*, detain those criminals!"

Whatever Siewert said next was drowned out by the massive guns of the Humboldthain flak tower. Max glanced up.

More searchlights blinked on, and the web of light was beginning to rake the sky.

"Mutti and Papa are awake now for sure!" he said to Gerta.

"We've got bigger problems!" she yelled in reply. "We have to get to a shelter!"

They ran faster. The *blockwart*'s heavy steps faded as the flak hammered the sky.

Papa always told them that if they were ever caught out in the open during a raid, all they had to do was follow the crowd—everybody would be headed to the nearest public shelter.

"There!" Max said. Across the street, people appeared to be milling about. It had to be the other scattered pedestrians, forming a ragged line. They took a sharp left. Max risked a quick glance over his shoulder. The *blockwart* was nowhere to be seen. Still, he did not feel any measure of relief. Getting away from Siewert now only meant that the Nazi would come for them later. He knew exactly who they were and where they lived.

But Gerta was right. They had bigger problems. First, they had to survive the bombs.

NINETEEN

The shelter that Max and Gerta found themselves in was a reinforced train tunnel on the border of Dahlem and the Grunewald forest. It was part of Berlin's *sofortprogramm*—emergency program—which resulted in the construction of three flak towers and five hundred public bunkers.

Max had never been inside a public shelter before. He was surprised to find that it was divided up into dozens of rooms, but also relieved—this would make it more difficult for Herr Siewert to track them down. The room they chose to settle in was sparsely furnished with wooden benches and a few bunks, which were already full of small children. There was a toilet in one corner, hidden behind a pair of wooden screens that could be opened and closed for privacy.

Bare electric bulbs were strung from a line of wire that ran the length of the ceiling, and the floors were dabbed with glowing blots of phosphorescent paint. Max thought of his classmate Joseph's description of the wall of paint that was supposedly bright enough to read by. The walls in this shelter were bare concrete, unpainted except for a slogan above the doorway:

Gehorche den Regeln. Hilfe deinen Nachbarn.

(Obey the rules. Help your neighbors.)

Max and Gerta sat down on the corner of a bench, squeezing into the only available space. All around the room, Berliners were calmly unpacking decks of cards, books, and newspapers. It would be hours before the all clear, and people had learned that it was better to keep busy than to sit and stare at the walls and listen to the bombs, wondering if they were coming closer or if it was just their imaginations.

Max removed his scarf and unbuttoned his coat, wincing at the pain in his shoulder. He was sweaty from the sudden flight from Herr Siewert. The air inside the shelter was musty and close, and he wondered if he ought to start cranking the hand-operated air pump that crouched like a robot from a science-fiction tale in the corner of the room.

The bunker muffled the air-raid siren, but Max could still hear it wailing thinly, like some trapped animal. The flak was a riot of dull bursts that he felt in his stomach.

He glanced at their neighbors on the bench—an elderly couple in pajamas and overcoats, sharing a newspaper.

He whispered to Gerta, "Do you think he followed us in here?"

"I don't know," she said. "He wouldn't want to be outside in a raid any more than we would, so he had to have gone to a shelter somewhere. And this was the closest one."

Max couldn't help but stare at the door, half expecting Siewert to burst through at any moment, a pair of Gestapo agents at his side. But there was only a little boy, younger than Max, who peeked in curiously until his mother shooed him along.

Seated on the bench on the opposite wall was a large family—Max counted four young children and two parents, along with a grandfather hunched like a carrion bird over his newspaper. The father dealt cards to each of the children, and Max felt a sudden pang of homesickness. Papa and Mutti would be frantic with worry, and it would probably be several hours before Max and Gerta could make their way home. He closed his eyes and prayed for this raid to be a false alarm. That way, the all clear would come much sooner.

But at that moment, the floor beneath his boots trembled. A quick hush swept across the room. The first bombs had slammed into the city. In the cellar at home, Max was an excellent judge of how far the bombs were falling from their villa. He could read the way the cellar rumbled and shook. It was like counting the seconds between lightning and thunder to pinpoint the distance of the storm. But here, everything was different—the depth of the shelter, the thickness of the walls, the sheer number of Berliners huddled together inside. For all he knew, the bombs could be falling right outside in Messelpark, or far away in Lichtenberg.

So much for a false alarm.

"I don't like it in here," Gerta said.

"It's not so bad," Max said.

"No, I mean, *here*—this room. There's only one door," she pointed out. "We're trapped."

A baby squalled and squirmed in its mother's arms. Max grimaced as its cries became high-pitched shrieks.

Suddenly, Max felt like he was being throttled by Herr Siewert's baton all over again. He crashed against Gerta, then swung hard the other way, nearly flinging himself off the bench. Others weren't so lucky—the old woman next to them was sprawled on the floor. Quickly, Gerta and Max helped her back to her seat.

Dust thickened the air. A pair of teenagers manned the air pump. An uneasy silence fell over the room. No question about it: That bomb had fallen close by. Max wondered if one of the bombers had strayed off course—it was a cloudy, moonless night, after all—or if this neighborhood was being targeted.

A feeling of great helplessness swept over him. He

remembered looking out of his bedroom window at the wave of bombers coming across the sky. The hugeness of war—the way it swallowed up millions of lives with its relentless appetite—made him feel like an ant on hot pavement, sizzling under a magnifying glass. There was nothing any of them could do but sit and wait.

The baby wailed like a banshee, the sound drilling into Max's skull. He closed his eyes.

"We're going to be okay," he said aloud, just to hear it spoken, to give it shape and truth.

Gerta put her arms around him and held him tight. "Bombs can't touch us," she said. "We're under the protection of the cave troll."

Max laughed. "You should have told me the cave troll was *good*. Then I wouldn't have been so scared of him."

"Where's the fun in that?"

Next to them, the elderly couple had folded up their newspaper. They were holding hands and staring at the ceiling, as if a stern gaze could ward off the bombs.

Max listened to the flak guns booming ceaselessly and pictured great silver birds cutting deadly swaths across a bloodred sky.

And then the world blinked out, and Max found himself tossed like a ship on a storm-wracked sea. In the darkness, all he knew was noise: screams of panic and the deafening shudder of a massive concrete collapse. Gerta was instantly wrenched away from him, and he flailed blindly, trying to find her hand. He thought he might be upside down—at the very least, he was not on his feet. He had the abrupt sensation of floating weightlessly for a moment, and then the breath whooshed from his lungs as he was mercilessly thrown back to earth.

Bright spots danced in the darkness, then resolved to an unsteady blur. *Fire*, he thought, but that didn't make any sense. There was no heat, just a cacophony of shouts and a vague awareness that the room had reshaped itself. He blinked, and the bright blur faded into the darkness. His head felt stuffed with cotton. He moved his limbs one by one and was greatly relieved to find them all intact.

He pushed himself up to his feet and winced at a sharp pain in his chest—a bruised rib, perhaps. All around him, he could make out dim shapes moving through the darkness, some crying out, some silent.

"Gerta!" he yelled, but what came out was a hoarse rasp. The room was thick with swirling dust. He coughed and spit a glob of grit and saliva. "Gerta!" he called again.

But it was no use. She would never hear him over the clamor of an entire shelter crying out for help.

Then he remembered his torch! He reached into his pocket, pulled it out, and clicked it on. The light wavered and then steadied itself, and he swept the beam around the room—or what was left of it. One wall looked like it had been rammed by a truck and caved in. It was now a pile of cracked cinder blocks and jagged chunks of cement. A skinny arm jutted out of the rubble, bent at an impossible angle. Max rushed over, got down on his knees, stuck the torch in his mouth, and began tossing aside bricks, scarcely noticing when a sharp edge sliced into his palm.

"Help!" he called out. "I need some help over here!"

As he worked, his mind spun frantically. The shelter had just been bombed, there was no doubt about that. But the shelter was massive. If this particular room had taken a direct hit, they would have been vaporized instantly, yanked out of existence. The bomb must have struck the opposite end of the shelter. What took down the wall was merely a shock wave, or the domino effect of the shelter's collapse.

Suddenly, another pair of hands began pulling chunks of cement from the pile. Max turned his head, and the beam of the torch fell upon his sister's face.

"Gerta!" he yelled, and the torch fell from his mouth. He grabbed it before it got lost in the rubble and aimed the beam at his sister. She was caked in gray dust, and her forehead was smeared with blood. Max didn't know if it was hers or someone else's.

"Maxi!" she cried. "I didn't know that was you. I was

afraid . . ." She trailed off. Together they worked to dislodge a massive piece of cement.

Gerta didn't have to finish her sentence. He'd had the same thought. *I was afraid that was you buried under the rubble.*

With all his remaining strength, Max shoved a cinder block off the pile. In the torchlight, an unblinking eye stared up at him, and surrounding the eye was the face of the old woman who had been sitting next to him on the bench. She was dead. There was no sign of her husband.

"Come on," Gerta said, pulling on his arm. "There's nothing we can do."

Max stood up, sweeping the beam across what remained of the room. The mother and father from the card-playing family were supporting the grandfather between them, staggering toward the door. Their children followed calmly, clasping hands—*Those kids have been well trained*, Max thought. He watched the parade of dusty faces, and his mind began to feel unmoored from his body. He felt like he was drifting through a strange film, where the dead rose and crept out of their underground tombs . . .

"Maxi," Gerta said, "we have to get out of these tunnels."

He snapped back to reality, and together they joined the procession. Outside, the narrow hallway was choked with panicked survivors. Light from a dozen torches danced and spun. There did not appear to be anyone in charge.

"This way!" Max led Gerta down the main corridor. How many rooms had they passed on the way in before they came to theirs? He didn't know, and anyway, it was impossible to count them. The blast had reduced many of the cement partitions to rubble, and piles of bricks obscured the phosphorescent paint on the floor.

Suddenly, Max felt a hand grab his ankle. A man's voice came out of the darkness, weak and faint. *"Help me."*

Max flicked the torchlight down to his feet. There was a meaty hand wrapped around his ankle, and attached to the hand was the *blockwart*, Herr Siewert. He was lying on his stomach, pinned underneath an enormous section of fallen wall.

"Max," Gerta said coldly. "Come on."

Max stood there, unsure of what to do. The *blockwart* was a Nazi who had just caught Max and Gerta delivering false papers to the Jewish underground. He was certainly going to turn the entire Hoffmann family over to the Gestapo as soon as he possibly could.

And yet—

By leaving him pinned underground in the ruins of the shelter, Max was condemning him to death. It seemed like it should be an easy choice—and maybe it was, for Gerta. But all Max could think about was that the hand around his ankle belonged to a living person, and he—Max Hoffmann—would be responsible for this living person's death. He would carry that weight for the rest of his life.

"I am very cold," Herr Siewert said softly, squinting into the light.

He doesn't know it's me, Max thought.

Herr Siewert began to cough and sputter. Blood dripped from his mouth and began to pool beneath him.

"Heil Hitler," Siewert muttered, and trailed off into nonsense.

"Hold this," Max said, handing his sister the torch. Then he gripped the massive, oblong chunk of cement and strained to lift it. The cement did not budge. It would take several people working together to dislodge it.

"Max," Gerta said wearily.

"I can't just leave him!" Max said. In his mind he saw the dead woman's eye, staring lifelessly up at him. How many people were lying dead in this shelter? And outside the shelter, in Berlin, how many hundreds or thousands more were dying?

If he could tip the tally of the dead back toward the living, even by one person, then wasn't it the right thing to do? Even if the person in question was Herr Siewert?

"It's him or us," Gerta said calmly.

Ignoring her, Max knelt down. Herr Siewert was muttering something about a uniform, and a march down Unter den

Linden. Blood was beginning to pool around his head. Max caught the man's eye, dull as a pebble.

"I'm going to get help," Max assured him. "Hang on."

Suddenly, Siewert's eye flashed with recognition. Max felt the man's grip tighten around his ankle.

"You!" Siewert rasped. Then he coughed, and Max turned away to avoid being splashed in the face with blood. Siewert whispered something that Max couldn't make out.

He's dying, thought Max.

"What did you say?" Max said. This might be the man's last words. Even Herr Siewert deserved to have somebody hear them.

"You," Siewert repeated, and paused to gather the strength to continue, "and your whole family will die in the camps. That is the fate of Jew-lovers and traitors."

With that, the last bit of light in his eyes blinked out. The grip on Max's ankle relaxed, and the hand fell away.

Max stood up. "He's gone."

"What did he say to you?"

Max shook his head and took back his torch. "Nothing. Let's get out of here."

TWENTY

The entrance to the shelter had partially collapsed. A human chain of rescue workers and firefighters pulled survivors out of the narrow opening one by one. When Max and Gerta finally emerged, they gulped down crisp night air, which tasted like the purest thing in the whole world after breathing the foul air of the shelter.

The sky glowed red to the east, on the other side of Messelpark, where a fire was burning out of control. To the west, ruins of the Grunewald train station smoldered. So that was what had happened—the station itself had taken a direct hit, and the pressure wave from the blast had rocketed through the tunnels below. Max shuddered to think what would have happened if a fire had raged through the shelter. A wall of flame tearing through the narrow corridors, scorching everything in its path, all those trapped Berliners roasted alive . . .

Max glanced up. While the searchlights still swept the sky,

the flak had gone quiet. The raid was over, the bombers returning to their bases in England.

Blue-tinted electric lanterns had been arranged in a semicircle around the collapsed entrance to the shelter. As the light mingled with the glow from the twin infernos, rescue workers moved grimly through a lavender night. Max and Gerta watched as limp bodies were pulled from the shelter and laid out side by side in the street. Gerta put her arms around her brother and held him tight. Max felt a curious dullness of spirit as the last of his adrenaline burned away. They had survived. Many others had died. There was a randomness to it all that he had not fully appreciated until this moment.

"How come we lived," Max said, "and the old lady died? She was sitting right next to me. If the wall had come down a little differently . . ."

"I honestly don't know," Gerta said. "Maybe it's because we still have a job to do." She patted the pocket of her coat.

Max's eyes widened. "Siewert didn't get the documents?"

"No. I crammed 'em down into my pocket as soon as he grabbed me. He didn't have a chance to search me before you charged him." She peered into his eyes. In the weird light, the blood on her forehead looked like a dark blob, a total absence of color. "That was very brave, Maxi. I don't know what would have happened if you hadn't done that."

Max didn't know what to say. This whole night, from the

time he heard Gerta's screams until the collapse of the shelter, Max hadn't felt very courageous. There hadn't been much time to feel anything at all, but now a sharp, animal fear settled in his guts. What were they doing, away from home during a raid, sneaking around Berlin at night with forged documents in their pockets?

He thought of Siewert's dying words. Oh, how he wished he could forget them.

It was all so far beyond his ability to deal with. Thoughts of home descended on him with a furious, teeth-grinding urgency. He wanted desperately to see the knights on his shelf, and to sit with Mutti reading on the sofa while Papa smoked his pipe.

"Let's go home," he said.

Gerta wiped blood from her forehead with the end of her scarf. "My thoughts exactly."

They headed west along Messelstrasse. There were many more pedestrians out now, as the night tilted toward dawn. Nobody could sleep anyway, Max figured. They might as well survey the damage.

"You know," Gerta said, "I think Siewert knew something was going to happen tonight. I think he was out keeping watch."

"That's sort of his job," Max said. At the same time he thought: *Was. That* was *his job.*

"Yeah," Gerta said thoughtfully. "I guess. It's just, when he grabbed me, the first thing he said was, *I've been waiting for you*. Like he knew we were going to be there."

Max could sense his sister's mind hatching a theory. He hoped she would wait until tomorrow to share it with him. He was too weary for an animated discussion. Of course, she didn't wait.

Gerta stopped abruptly and grabbed the sleeve of his jacket. "What if there's a spy, Maxi?"

"*Shhhh,*" he said, glancing around at the dark houses. They had turned onto a street that was untouched by the bombs, but Max was sure that behind darkened windows sleepless Berliners paced, listening to the street.

Gerta lowered her voice. "Who are the people who know about our dead drops?"

Reluctantly, Max played along. "Frau Becker. Albert. The princess."

"Hans," Gerta said. "General Vogel."

"And Herr Trott," Max said darkly, thinking of the glowering factory owner's scarred face. "Let's keep moving." Knowing Gerta, she was capable of standing on the sidewalk for twenty minutes while her mind turned over all the possibilities.

The searchlights vanished as they walked beneath the camouflage netting, and Max suddenly felt like somebody was squeezing his neck. He gasped for air. It was Herr Siewert's cold dead hand, creeping out of the night to choke him.

All at once, he was back in the shelter, breathing in dust and smoke in the chaotic darkness, bashed this way and that, unsure which way was up.

Deep breaths, Max, he thought. While he regained his composure, Gerta kept up her feverish whispering.

"—who would have the most to gain by betraying the group?" she was saying.

"I don't know, Gerta," Max said wearily. It was too dizzying for him to think about right now—a spy for the Nazis in Frau Becker's cozy sitting room.

No. Gerta was just being paranoid. Frau Becker knew every little thing that happened in Berlin. Surely she could sniff out a spy in her midst.

"I think right now we should be more worried about Mutti and Papa," he said.

This silenced Gerta for a moment. She sighed. "You're right. They've probably got searchers with dogs out looking for us."

"Maybe they'll be so happy to see us that they'll forget to be mad."

Gerta scoffed. "Have you *met* our mother, Maxi?" She paused. "We need to get our stories straight. We need a plan."

"No, Gerta!" Max said, taken aback by his own vehemence. "No more schemes, no more plans. Let's just go home and tell them what happened." He could feel tears forming. The old woman's dead, sightless eye was burned into his mind. His ankle felt clammy and wrong where Siewert had gripped it. He could taste the dust and smoke of the shelter, hear the cries of the injured and the terrified.

"Okay," Gerta said quietly. "No more schemes."

TWENTY-ONE

The house was dark and quiet. Max turned his key and opened the door. Gerta followed and shut the door behind them. Max crept across the living room. There was a strange atmosphere in the room—a feeling of total absence—and for a moment he thought they'd blundered into a neighbor's house. He pulled the switch on the lamp. Nothing.

"They must have turned off the electricity for the raid, and then never bothered to turn it back on," Gerta said, heading for the main switch in the back of the coat closet. It was her job to cut the electricity at the start of every raid, and she knew the way in the dark. A moment later, the lamp came to life.

"Papa?" Max called out. He took off his scarf and jacket and let them fall to the floor, too tired to hang them up. He wished both his parents were here to yell at him and send him to bed. Anything to get to the "bed" part of this crazy night faster would be fine with him. He felt like a poor-quality version of himself, a copy of a copy. The only way to feel like normal Max Hoffmann again would be a long, uninterrupted sleep.

Preferably one without any dreams.

He listened to his sister open the cellar down and call down into the shelter. No reply.

"Nobody's here," she said, coming back to the living room.

"I'm going to bed," Max said, heading for the stairs. "I'm asleep on my feet. They can wake me up to yell at me if they want."

Before he took three steps, the front door opened and his parents burst inside. With a sharp cry, Mutti rushed over to Max and corralled him in an embrace. At the same time, she dragged him over to Gerta so she could squeeze them together and smother their faces with kisses. She smelled like ash and the cold night air.

After what felt like a full minute, she let them go. Her eyes were wet, and she wiped them on her sleeve.

"When the sirens went off and you weren't in your rooms, I thought . . ." She shook her head, smiling through her tears. "I don't know what I thought."

"We thought we would never see you again," Papa said bluntly. He came slowly into the living room and sat down on the sofa. His face was pale and drawn. He looked from Max to Gerta as if he couldn't believe his eyes. "It is so difficult, in these times, not to imagine the worst."

Before Max's eyes, his father seemed to deflate. He had never seen Papa so tired and drained before, not even after spending two whole days at the hospital without sleep treating Berlin's wounded.

"We're sorry," Max said quietly. On top of everything else jostling for space in his mind tonight—the shelter's collapse, the *blockwart*'s dying threat—he felt like he'd stolen some of his father's vitality away with his choice to sneak out. Karl Hoffmann looked like he'd aged ten years in a single night.

"We were just trying to help," Gerta said. "If we didn't get caught in the raid, we would've been home before you—"

"My God, Gerta, your face!" And just like that, Max's father leaped from the couch and into his old self. "Ingrid, get me my bag, please."

Mutti hurried away down the hall.

Gerta took a step back. "I'm fine, Papa, really." She slid her hand across her forehead, wiping away blood, then showed her palm to her father. "It's not mine."

"We ran to a public shelter when we heard the sirens," Max said, "just like you told us."

"It got hit," Gerta said.

"And part of it collapsed," Max said as Mutti returned with the bag. Quickly, he filled his parents in on some of the details—finding their way out of the ruins, Herr Siewert's demise, the bodies pulled from the wreckage of the shelter.

"My God!" Mutti said. "You are lucky to be alive." She tossed the bag on the sofa and gathered Max and Gerta up for another long embrace. "What on earth were you doing out after midnight in the first place?"

Gerta reached into her pocket and pulled out a small paper square—the identification documents from Frau Becker, neatly folded.

"A dead drop over by Messelpark," she said.

Mutti's expression hardened. She snatched the documents from Gerta's hand and shot Papa a fierce look. "I'm going to boil that old woman's head!"

"It was our idea," Max admitted. "We went to her house after school and asked for another job."

"*Karl*," Mutti said.

"Ingrid," he replied thoughtfully. He lit his pipe with calm, steady hands, and regarded his children with curiosity, as if seeing them for the first time.

"That was a very disobedient thing to do," he said. "For that, I am disappointed in you both."

Max looked down at the floor.

"It was also very brave," Papa said.

Max's eyes snapped back up.

"As much as your mother and I would like to keep you close to us every second of the day, that is not the reality of life during this infernal war. And if we are ever going to outlast these Nazi dogs, we will need brave young people to lead us into the future. People like you, Gerta. And you, Max."

"So," Gerta said, "we're not in trouble?"

Mutti let out a quick laugh—more like a snort. "Oh, daughter, of course you're in trouble. Even brave children of the resistance can still be grounded—war or no war. From now until Christmas, you are to leave this house for school only, and you are to go straight there and come directly home afterward. No Frau Becker, no candy shops, no cinemas. If you disobey these rules, the terms will be extended into the new year."

"But—" Gerta began to protest. Papa cut her off.

"*But* nothing," he said. "Your mother is absolutely correct. And instead of those American film magazines, you two will select books from the shelves in the study to occupy yourselves."

"Those are Gerta's magazines," Max said. "I don't even read them."

"Both of you will stay inside and read books," Mutti said firmly. "That is the point."

"Now," Papa said, "I'm going to examine your cuts and bruises, and then you're going to go to bed."

"I think we could *all* use some sleep," Mutti said.

Papa shook his head. "Not me. I must go to the hospital. Haven't you heard?" He looked wearily at the faces of his wife and children. "A shelter collapsed near Messelpark."

TWENTY-TWO

December slid past like a reel of film unspooling, a blur of snowy afternoons and long, dull evenings indoors. Max found that he was beginning to have trouble sleeping. He would often wake with his sheets twined around his legs, sweat soaking the mattress, swatting Herr Siewert's dead hands away from his ankles. Or else he would dream of the old woman's eye, and the cries of the trapped and wounded would swirl around him like banshees on the wind.

He wondered how Papa, who witnessed more horrors every day than the rest of them would see in their lifetimes, managed to sleep so soundly at night. Maybe he had simply grown accustomed to working among the dead and the dying.

Maybe he was simply exhausted.

Mutti and Papa refused to tell Max and Gerta anything about the fate of the documents they were supposed to drop by Messelpark. And they were equally tight-lipped about the plot to kill Hitler. Max wondered if Frau Becker had approved a plan of action yet, and where the attempt would be carried out. He saw those maps in his dreams sometimes, too—Wolf's Lair, Eagle's Nest, Führerbunker—and thought of the Becker Circle's mysterious "counterparts" as rugged men and beautiful women in far-flung parts of the world, meeting furtively in cafés in Morocco and ducking into alleyways in Prague. He yearned to be a part of it all again. Maybe not so much the dead drops—he'd had enough of those for one war. He simply wanted to visit Frau Becker's sumptuous living room, eat Hans's chocolates, listen to the princess describe far-fetched assassination techniques.

As for Gerta, she sustained herself through the long weeks by nurturing her theory of the Nazi spy in the Becker Circle. She held whispered conferences with Max nearly every day, examining the suspects from every angle. Max played along, just for something to do, but he still wasn't convinced. They didn't have much evidence besides the words that Herr Siewert had spoken when he thought he was apprehending them. But Gerta seemed to thrive on the intrigue—one day she'd come bursting into his room, convinced it had to be General Vogel, and the next day she'd be equally fervent about the princess, or Hans.

Then, three days before Christmas, they received word from the Eastern Front.

Uncle Friedrich was dead—killed in a Soviet rocket attack in the besieged city of Stalingrad, where much of the Wehrmacht's Sixth Army was surrounded. He had been killed instantly—blown to bits along with twenty-seven fellow soldiers in an ambush along a snowy ridge.

The last time Max had seen his uncle, Friedrich had brought him his favorite figurine, his knight on horseback.

Cavalry is the jewel of any fighting force, his uncle had told him. *Once upon a time, it was horses. Now we have tanks.*

Do the Soviets have tanks, too? Max had asked. Of course he knew that they did, but he liked to keep his uncle talking. Friedrich was a jovial man who reminded Max of a traveling storyteller from a vanished world, spinning epic yarns in the courtyard of some rambling old castle.

Tanks as far as the eye can see, Maxi. His eyes twinkled. *But ours are much quicker! Our cavalry is made up of stallions. The Soviets have old, swaybacked pack mules.*

Max had not seen Uncle Friedrich since the summer of 1941, at the very beginning of Operation Barbarossa—the invasion of the Soviet Union, which was by now becoming a full-scale military disaster for Germany. The Wehrmacht was on a mad retreat across a barren, wintry tundra, pursued and harassed by a massive Soviet army thirsty for vengeance.

In his bedroom, Max turned his favorite knight over in his hand, worrying at it like a string of prayer beads. He imagined

Uncle Friedrich whittling a new piece for his collection—
clumsily, awkwardly, hands frozen and cracked from the
cold—and storing it in his pack, waiting until his homecom-
ing when he could give it to his nephew. Now those skilled
hands would never make another figurine. Never make anything at all.

He imagined Uncle Friedrich waking up, huddled in a
trench, on the morning of the ambush. Was there part of him
that knew, deep down, that this would be his last day on
earth?

Max hoped not. He hoped that Uncle Friedrich had been
thinking of home when the rockets came screaming in.

As for Mutti, she mourned the loss of her older brother by
throwing herself into Christmas preparations. She spent two
days scouring the black market, and finally came home with
the main ingredient for the Hoffmanns' traditional Christmas
Eve meal of carp, which she filleted and fried to crispy
perfection.

It had been Uncle Friedrich's favorite dish.

Afterward, the Hoffmanns joined some of their neighbors
for caroling on the streets of Dahlem, Max and Gerta shielding
their candles with gloved hands to keep them from going out.

They were on the second verse of "Silent Night" when the
air-raid siren drove them all back inside.

Our counterparts want options," Frau Becker said. "And I don't blame them. Too much can go wrong to settle for one plan. We may have to move quickly, to strike when the opportunity presents itself. And so we must be prepared."

It was January of 1944, a week of dismal snow flurries and leaden skies that made it feel as if Berlin were floating in a massive cloud, untethered from the rest of Germany. That morning, Max's parents had surprised him by telling him to take a bath—the Hoffmanns were going to a meeting of the Becker Circle.

Max had all but given up hope of ever seeing the conspirators again. *Why now?* he wondered as he popped one of Hans's chocolates into his mouth. The Swiss medical student had managed to smuggle an entire bag of foil-wrapped bonbons into Berlin, and he dumped them all out on Frau Becker's dining table as if he were presenting gold doubloons to a pirate king.

Besides the chocolates, Albert—dressed as a shabby beggar—set out pickled herring, potato pancakes, pork schnitzel, and a hot apple strudel that Max had been eyeing since they walked in.

"It smacks of indecision," General Vogel said. He was sitting on the sofa clutching a glass of champagne in his bearlike paw. "And it leaves us spread too thin."

"I agree," Hans said, from the arm of the plush chair in which the princess was sprawled. "If we had a singular focus, we could dedicate all our resources to it. Not pick away at the problem from so many different angles." He glanced at Papa. "We should be more surgical."

"Nevertheless," Frau Becker said, "our counterparts are assuming a greater share of the risk, as they will be the ones to actually carry out the assassination. And so we must serve their needs as best we can."

"In Russia before the revolution," the princess said, "the czar's personal bodyguard would carry out political assassinations with bullets of ice, which would melt and leave no evidence."

"Ice bullets," Hans said. "Wonderful. Our work here is done."

The princess shrugged and sipped her tea.

Max glanced over to the fireplace, where Herr Trott stood with his arms crossed, staring silently into the flames.

"The issue is access," Frau Becker said. "Access to Hitler requires a thorough knowledge of his whereabouts—knowledge that is more difficult now than it was even a month ago, and it grows more difficult every day. He is suspicious of crowds, even of Berlin itself. The man spends most of his time in the Wolf's Lair, where no one but his innermost circle is allowed."

"It's easy to be at the head of a rally in the Sportpalast while the war is going well," General Vogel said. "But now that we're waiting for the Allied invasion in the west and the Red Army's routing us in the east, he doesn't dare show his face in public. He cowers in his lair." He shook his head and appeared visibly ill. "So many lives in the hands of a single madman . . ."

"I heard he's addicted to morphine," the princess offered.

"Amphetamines," growled Herr Trott without turning around. "His personal doctor injects him every morning."

"If that's true," Papa said, "he will only grow more manic. The drugs will feed his insanity."

"And that is precisely why we must act now," said an unfamiliar voice. All heads turned as a man in an immaculate black overcoat burst through the velvet curtain and into the sitting room.

At first, Max thought it was Albert in yet another disguise. But that notion vanished when Albert appeared beside the stranger to take his coat and retreat back into the hallway.

The newest visitor to Frau Becker's sitting room was tall and imposing, with an almost regal bearing. As soon as he walked in, the atmosphere of the room seemed to shift, as if he drew the attention of not only the guests but the furniture itself. *Aristocrat*, Max thought at once. And judging by the crisp uniform, an army officer, too. Even the man's obvious injuries—he was missing his right hand, two fingers of his left, and he wore an eye patch over his left eye—did nothing to diminish his stature.

General Vogel crossed the room and shook the man's remaining hand. "Claus!" he said. "Wonderful to see you."

The man gave a slight bow. "And you, as always, Lothar."

Max had never seen high-ranking officers address each other by their first names before.

Frau Becker pointed her cane at the new guest. "May I introduce our most illustrious counterpart on the military side, Colonel Claus von Stauffenberg."

Claus bowed again. "Thank you, Frau Becker." He addressed the gathered conspirators. "I wanted to come in person to express my admiration for your efforts on behalf of the resistance. I know it can feel like thankless work, in the face of overwhelming odds, but as the great poet Goethe once wrote, *knowing is not enough; we must apply. Willing is not enough; we must take action.*"

"I believe it is, more simply, *willing is not enough; we must do*," the princess said.

Hans cleared his throat.

Claus grinned. "You are correct, of course. Princess Marie Vasiliev, I presume. Pleasure to make your acquaintance."

"And yours, Count," the princess said. *Count*, Max thought. So that confirmed it: Claus von Stauffenberg was definitely from an old, noble family—just like Frau Becker.

"Have some cake," Frau Becker said.

Claus shook his head. "I'm afraid, since my injuries, I have no stomach for sweets."

Max found himself moving toward the colonel, as if drawn by some invisible tether. "I'm Max," he said, and gestured over his shoulder. "That's my sister, Gerta."

"Ah!" Claus's good eye lit up. "Frau Becker has told me all about you. You should know that when things feel hopeless, brave comrades like you and your sister inspire me to keep fighting. Truly."

Goose bumps broke out down Max's arms. "N-nice to meet you," he stammered. He had heard stories from people who'd met Hitler at the beginning of the war, when the Führer was bursting with power and prestige. They described his presence in almost mythical terms, as if they were being drawn to some ancient force beyond human understanding. Max thought he finally understood what they were talking about. This man, Claus von Stauffenberg, had a similar magnetism. Yet Hitler's eyes were an eerie, watery blue, while Claus's one good eye shone with determination and clarity, like a brilliant sky reflected on the surface of the Spree.

"It's always nice to see the younger generation so enthusiastic about committing high treason with me," Claus said.

There was a moment of silence. Then Herr Trott roared with laughter. Claus tried to keep a straight face, but a smile broke through. Hans doubled over, cackling madly, and the princess spit her tea back into her teacup.

Here was another key difference between Claus von Stauffenberg and Adolf Hitler, Max thought. The army colonel had a sense of humor.

"All right, all right." Frau Becker waved her cane in the air. "Enough levity for one war. Now, Claus, what do you need from us?"

"I need you to be prepared for the aftermath of the assassination," Claus said, glancing quickly at everyone in turn. "Make no mistake: The hours and days following Hitler's death will be chaotic. And, if I may speak frankly—full of uncertainty."

"You have narrowed down a course of action, then?" Frau Becker said.

"Yes," Claus said. "The Wehrmacht is to be issued new uniforms. A new, warmer design for the Eastern Front."

"Not a moment too soon," General Vogel said darkly. "Just in time for the retreat."

"I have arranged a demonstration of the new uniforms for our beloved Führer," Claus said. "A man I trust—a young lieutenant who shares our point of view—will model them for

Hitler himself. Underneath his uniform, he will be strapped with bombs. When he moves to embrace the Führer, he will detonate them—blowing Hitler away."

"And killing himself," Mutti said.

Claus did not falter. "Yes, Frau Hoffmann. He will be a martyr for the resistance."

The princess clapped wildly. "A fashion show assassination! I approve wholeheartedly, Count."

"Thank you, Princess. I have been attempting to arrange it for months, but Hitler is not easy to pin down, as you well know. Finally, he has agreed to the second week in February. The afternoon of the tenth."

Claus went on to explain what would happen after Hitler was dead—how the army officers loyal to the cause of the resistance would turn on the SS and disarm them, and how a new, provisional government would quickly form to fill the void left by the Nazis.

"What's it called?" Max said after Claus was finished speaking.

Claus frowned. "I'm sorry—what is *what* called, Max?"

"The plot! It has to have a code name, right?"

"Ah, yes. Quite right," Claus said. "Our little conspiracy does indeed have a name." He paused. "We call it Operation Valkyrie."

TWENTY-FOUR

FEBRUARY 10, 1944

The Hoffmanns gathered around their radio. Affixed to the tuning dial, by order of the *blockwart*, was a red card that said:

Remember: Listening to foreign broadcasts is an offense against the national security of our people. By order of the Führer, it will be punished with severe custodial sentences.

Max remembered the day that Herr Siewert had given them the card and personally supervised as Papa attached it to the dial. Of course, Gerta had wanted to rip it off the minute Herr Siewert shut the door behind him, but Papa thought it was safer to leave it alone. The *blockwart* was the kind of man who would come over unannounced to make sure that the card was still displayed in its proper place.

Not anymore, Max thought. And suddenly the night of the shelter's collapse closed in around him, and the living room was a smoking ruin, and a little girl was screaming, and a dead eye stared at him from out of the darkness . . .

He shoved the memories aside. He was getting better at ignoring them, but it was troubling how they could claw at him without warning at any time, day or night.

"I bet the Nazis won't even tell us when Hitler's dead," Gerta said. "I bet they'll pretend like it didn't happen for as long as they can."

"Oh, I am certain Goebbels will manage to finesse it," Mutti said.

"In death, our beloved and fearless Führer only grows more powerful," Papa intoned, impersonating the voice of the Nazi propaganda minister. "We await his return on his winged horse to lead our holy army to victory."

Max laughed. He loved to see his parents like this: giddy with tension and anticipation, but also with long-buried joy so ready to erupt, it was already leaking out.

Mutti turned the tuning dial, and Max was treated to a rapid-fire tour of German radio: the *volksmusik* (people's music) tune "Glocken der Heimat" (Bells of the Homeland), with its syrupy strings. The melancholy longing of "Lili Marleen." The soaring, martial triumph that Max recognized instantly as one of Wagner's operas, which reminded him of Nazi boots marching in lockstep down the street.

Finally, Mutti stopped at a newsman's voice droning on about how the German collapse on the Eastern Front was, in reality, a "strategic retreat," and that instead of racing back to Germany with the Red Army in pursuit, what the Wehrmacht was actually doing was "shortening the lines."

Mutti's expression hardened. "Millions dead, the Allies closing in on all sides, and still the Nazis can't speak the truth to the people of Berlin. What will they say when the entire city is ash?"

"They will call it 'strategic rebuilding,'" Papa said.

Gerta caught Max's eye and puffed out her cheeks, pursed her lips, and made her eyes bulge.

"Back to the cellar with you, cave troll!" Max said. "I banish thee in the name of the Becker Circle."

Gerta held her breath until her face turned scarlet, then let the air rush out.

"Shh!" Papa said, and leaned closer to the radio. A different newscaster interrupted the first with a special report from the Eastern Front.

"*The Fifth SS Panzer Division has made a valiant stand at the*

Dnieper line, repeatedly fighting off Red Army advances despite the Soviets' superior numbers—"

"Ach," Mutti said, waving her hand dismissively toward the radio.

As if conjured by her wave, the telephone began to ring. Max's heart sank. It was always the hospital on the other end of the line, frantic with some emergency or another, begging Herr Doktor Hoffmann to come in.

Papa muttered something under his breath and went into the kitchen to answer the phone.

"The consolidation of our forces in the east is proving to be a great success . . . ," the radio said.

Papa returned a moment later. Max could tell by his grim expression that the news was not going to be good.

"That was Frau Becker," Papa said. "Hitler canceled the fashion show at the last minute. Nobody knows why."

"What do you mean *canceled*?" Max blurted out.

Mutti turned the radio off. Papa settled heavily into the sofa and sighed. "What I mean is, the Führer refused to show up. Apparently no explanation was provided."

"I swear," Mutti said, "that man is blessed with the devil's own luck."

"I don't think it was luck," Gerta said.

Papa raised an eyebrow.

Gerta took a deep breath, and Max readied himself for the torrent of words. He knew exactly what his sister was going to say. This was the chance she'd been waiting for.

"Back in December," Gerta said, "the night of our last dead drop and the shelter collapse, Herr Siewert said something to me when he caught me—*I've been waiting for you*, like he knew something was going to happen, and he was keeping watch."

"It was his job to keep watch over the neighborhood," Mutti pointed out.

Max chimed in. "That's what I said." He glanced at Gerta. "That it didn't really prove anything. But now, after this—"

"There has to be a spy in the Becker Circle!" Gerta said. "Somebody who knew that we were going to be near Messelpark that night! Somebody who got word to Hitler that the fashion show was a trap!"

"Lower your voice, Gerta," Mutti said.

Gerta's face was flushed with excitement. She had been turning her theories over in her mind for weeks, letting them simmer, and now that she was finally voicing them, she could barely contain her glee.

"Ingrid," Papa said.

"Karl," Mutti said. They looked at each other for a few seconds, and Max tried to read their expressions. But whatever passed between them was a mystery, transmitted in a language only they could understand.

"I suppose it is possible," Karl admitted after a moment. "The Gestapo knows how to apply pressure. If they have turned someone in our group into the Nazis' eyes and ears, it will be disastrous." He looked at his wife and his children in turn. "For all of us."

"Are you going to tell Frau Becker?" Max said.

"Yes," Papa said. "I will inform her of your suspicions."

"But what if she's the spy!" Gerta cried. "How do we know we can trust her?"

"Shh!" Mutti said.

"What if she's a secret Nazi?" Gerta whispered.

"Frau Becker is *not* a Nazi," Max countered. He felt like it was his duty to defend Frau Becker's honor. "She hates the Nazis. Think about what Albert told us—"

"What if Albert's the spy!" Gerta said.

Max paused to consider this. It was actually a pretty good guess. A man who could change his appearance at will would certainly make an excellent spy. He thought about how easily Albert's lie about the French machine gun at the Somme taking his arm sprang to his lips. Albert was such a slippery figure—who knew what was in the heart of a man like that?

"If Frau Becker is a Nazi," Mutti said, "she is the best actress I have ever seen."

"If Frau Becker is a Nazi," Papa said, "then we are already found out, and it is only a matter of time before the Gestapo come knocking at our door. But I simply do not believe that a woman like that has become such a firm believer in the Nazi cause that she would go to great lengths to put together a resistance movement, with the sole purpose of betraying it. Besides, we have no choice—we must bring this to her attention."

Mutti turned to Gerta. "Do you agree?"

Gerta blinked, taken aback by the question. She hesitated, then nodded. "Yes. I think she needs to know."

"And, Max," Mutti said, "what do you think?"

"What will Frau Becker do?" he asked, wondering if this would mean the end of the Becker Circle. How could they continue their salons in the sitting room, knowing that someone in their midst could be reporting all their secret, treasonous, punishable-by-death plans to the Nazis?

"I don't know," Papa admitted.

"I think we have to tell her, either way," Max said. "We can't just pretend this isn't happening."

Mutti nodded. "Then it's settled. We will speak to Frau Becker."

Max was relieved, but there was a troubling thought lodged in the back of his mind. He caught Gerta's eye and was sure that she was thinking the same thing.

Would they ever see Frau Becker again?

TWENTY-FIVE

As it turned out, Max and Gerta would see Frau Becker much sooner than they'd thought. The next morning, while Max was getting ready for school, Mutti knocked on his door.

"Hurry up and get dressed, Maxi. Then come downstairs."

Max frowned. He wasn't running late. Why was his mother being so pushy? Quickly, he laced up his shoes and bounded down the stairs. Gerta was already dressed and waiting in the living room, along with Papa and Mutti.

"Come," Papa said, gesturing toward the door. "We're going to take a ride."

"What about school?" Max said.

"School will just have to wait," Mutti said, ushering them outside into the frosty morning. A radiant blue sky stretched across Berlin, marred only by a dark plume rising from distant Friedrichshain, last night's bombing target. They hadn't even felt the tremors in Dahlem.

Max was astonished to find a shiny black Mercedes-Benz idling in front of their house. It was the car of a high-ranking official—most ordinary Berliners could never have afforded such a vehicle.

Max was rooted to the steps of the porch, staring at the car's darkly tinted windows, when the driver's-side door opened and a man in a Nazi uniform got out.

Max turned to bolt back into the house, but stopped when he felt his father's steady hand on his shoulder.

"Look closer," his father said quietly.

The driver of the Mercedes gave a crisp German salute, along with a sly wink. It was Albert, dressed in a perfect replica of a Nazi staff driver's uniform. His face was pale and gaunt, and his cheekbones seemed altered. Albert opened the passenger door and beckoned for the Hoffmanns to enter.

Max supposed they were just going to have to trust him.

Inside the car, a pair of leather bench-style seats faced each other. Frau Becker was seated on the bench at the rear. Her legs were wrapped in a thick woolen blanket, and her small, delicate upper body was bundled into a parka suitable for the Eastern Front. She wore Princess Marie's *ushanka*, which slipped down low on her forehead and nearly covered her eyes.

The Hoffmanns squeezed together on the bench across from her. Albert shut the door behind them, and a moment later the engine rumbled to life and the car slid smoothly into the street.

"Until this business with the rat in our henhouse is settled," Frau Becker said, "I'd rather not discuss any matters of importance in my home. Walls have ears, as they say."

Max thought of last week's *Hornet and Wasp* episode, where the crime-fighting duo uncovered hidden listening devices inside the prime minister's residence in London.

"You think you're being *bugged*?" Gerta said.

"Can't be too careful," Frau Becker said. "Well, unless you're my mother, I suppose. Poor woman was so afraid of germs after the poison gas attacks from our first go-round at a world war, she refused to come out of her bedroom for eleven years. I guess the apple didn't fall too far from the tree." She inhaled sharply. "Been a while since I've smelled the air out here." She wrinkled her nose. "Smells like rot."

To Max, it smelled like rich leather. He had never been inside a car that had built-in sliding curtains to cover the windows. Frau Becker kept them closed, as if she still couldn't bear to witness what had become of her beloved city.

"Now," she said to Max and Gerta, "tell me what happened, and please don't leave anything out."

Max opened his mouth, but before he could say a word,

Gerta rushed to fill the old woman in on the incident with Herr Siewert that had ignited her suspicions—suspicions that had been confirmed, in Gerta's mind, by Hitler's abrupt cancellation of the fashion show.

When she finished speaking, Frau Becker was silent. Lost in thought, she regarded the Hoffmanns with an inscrutable gaze, then slid her curtain aside to peer out at Berlin. Max wasn't sure what neighborhood they were in, but he caught a glimpse of a firefighting team snaking a massive hose into a pile of rubble. That meant there were survivors trapped inside the ruins, running out of oxygen. If the rescue crew could pump in fresh air, the people buried alive might stand a chance.

Frau Becker closed the curtain and leaned her head back against the seat.

"You may not know it to look at me now, but I loved to dance in Clärchens Ballhaus. This was such a joyful place, once upon a time . . ." She trailed off. Then she leaned forward. "If there are Nazis in our midst, they will find my sense of mercy sorely tested. We will root them out and kill them."

Frau Becker tightened her grip on her cane until her knuckles turned white. "This stays between us," she said. "Understood?" The Hoffmanns murmured their assent.

"Now then. When it comes to rooting out our rat, I admit that I am at a loss. If anyone has any ideas, I would be grateful." She lifted her cane. "The floor is open, ladies and gentlemen."

Max almost blurted out, *Have Herr Trott followed*, but managed to keep his mouth shut. It wouldn't do to go accusing members of the Becker Circle in front of Frau Becker herself, especially when he had no hard evidence.

"We plant false information," Papa said. "It's the only way to be sure. We give separate falsehoods to each member individually. That way, when the Nazis act on the information, we will know who our rat is."

"That might work if we had the resources of an entire spy agency at our disposal," Frau Becker said. "But we have only the people in this car. And we don't have eyes or ears inside the Gestapo or the SS."

"What about the dead drops?" Max said. Papa's suggestion had given him an idea. "That's how they almost caught us before—I think they'd jump at the chance to do it again."

"Absolutely not," Mutti said. "You will not be used as bait in some spy-catching scheme."

"Maxi," Gerta said, "you're a genius. Frau Becker, can you—"

"Gerta Hoffmann!" Mutti said sharply. But she had nothing to follow it up with—no reprimand, no admonishment. They had all come so far, it was absurd to forbid Max and his sister to participate in further resistance activities. It struck Max that bodies and buildings weren't the only things warped and changed by war. Even if they all survived, their family would never be the same.

"Can you set up four new dead drops?" Gerta asked Frau Becker. "It's like Papa said—we have to feed the false information to each person separately. So for the first drop, you only tell General Vogel where it's supposed to happen. For the next one, the princess."

"The third, Hans, and the fourth, Herr Trott," Frau Becker said. "Hmm. That way, if any of those drops are compromised, we will be able to trace a direct link back to our spy."

Mutti glared at Frau Becker. "I have permitted you to use my children as you see fit, and I have not slept more than two or three hours a night since we brought them into the group. But this—this is too much."

"Ingrid," Papa said softly.

"*Karl,*" she said.

"We're not being used," Max said.

"We're doing our part," Gerta said.

"Mutti, we want to help," Max said.

"We're just going to find a way to do it anyway," Gerta said.

"There you have it," Frau Becker said. "I promise you, Albert will be with you every step of the way. You may not see him, but rest assured he will be there. If there is trouble,

I pity the Gestapo inspector who comes up against Albert on a dark street."

At this, Max's pulse quickened. Albert in disguise, stalking him from the shadows. Gestapo agents, ready to pounce. Herr Siewert's dying words echoed in his head.

You and your whole family will die in the camps.

Maybe Mutti was right—maybe this was too much for them.

Then he caught the fierce gleam in Frau Becker's eye and banished the thought. The plot to kill Hitler was at stake! He pushed his fear to the back of his mind, but could not make it vanish entirely. There it throbbed, cold and dark, waiting to strike again.

He wondered if Uncle Friedrich had experienced fear like this on the Eastern Front—like a stalking monster, stealing away his ability to think, to act.

Of course, Max would never get the chance to ask him.

"Does anyone have a better idea?" Frau Becker looked from Mutti to Papa. After a long silence, she clapped her hands. "Then it's settled. The first drop will be tomorrow night, in Spandau. I will inform General Vogel and no one else."

"Karl," Mutti said wearily.

"Ingrid," Papa said, and placed his hand upon her knee.

"You'll need this." Frau Becker reached deep into the creases of her blanket and produced a tightly folded packet, similar to the forged documents that Max and Gerta had delivered back in December.

Max shot Gerta a quizzical look. Why did Frau Becker have these papers ready? Had she known exactly what the plan was going to be before she got in the car? Why, then, had she asked for suggestions?

Gerta shrugged and took the packet.

At that moment, the car rolled to a stop. Max pushed the curtain aside. They were outside their villa. It was as if Albert had known exactly how long the conversation was going to take, and planned his route perfectly.

Max just shook his head. There were so many things about the old woman and her servant that he would never, ever understand.

TWENTY-SIX

The gables and spires of the Old Spandau neighborhood crowded the evening sky. Max moved quickly along Lindenufer, past the ruins of the synagogue that the Nazis destroyed on Kristallnacht, way back in 1938. The years between then and now hadn't treated Spandau much better. Bombing raids had reduced entire blocks to rubble, and there was a furtive, broken-down melancholy to the few pedestrians he passed.

Across the street, Gerta popped in and out of the shadows. She kept her eyes down and walked like she belonged there. Max wished he could move with her quiet confidence. He still could not get over the feeling that everyone was watching him.

It was ridiculous, he knew. Besides, all he had to do was chalk a few words on some bricks. A man like Claus von Stauffenberg had to plan and carry out the assassination of the Führer himself, and yet the one time Max had met him, the colonel had acted like it was just another task, like planning a staff meeting or a luncheon. He had even joked about it!

It's always nice to see the younger generation so enthusiastic about committing high treason with me.

Max wondered if war had made the man who he was, or if he had always been that way. Was it possible to be born brave?

Max turned the corner, catching a glimpse of the Havel River through the trees to the east. At the same time, the fine hairs on the back of his neck prickled. Now he *knew* he was being watched, and spun abruptly on his heels to look behind him.

There was no one there.

Albert? he thought. Frau Becker's jack-of-all-trades servant was supposed to be here somewhere, keeping an eye on them. Max supposed he could be anyone—even the slender lady in the wide-brimmed hat and fur coat coming toward him. He caught her eye as she passed, along with a whiff of her perfume, and wondered.

When he reached the bombed-out apartment block on the corner, he took the chalk from his pocket, glanced around to make sure he was alone, and scrawled the coded phrase on a prominent brick.

Jürgen, Liesl and I are unhurt

His whole body tingled as he wrote. He felt like he was hovering above the sidewalk, and his head felt three sizes too big. What if General Vogel was the spy? There might be a Gestapo agent crouching in the rubble with his pistol drawn, ready to spring forth. How far away was Albert?

He put the chalk back into his pocket, threw a quick nod at Gerta across the street, and kept walking west. It wasn't until he reached the monument to Joachim II, several blocks away, that he realized he had been holding his breath. He let it out and took a moment to gather himself.

It was done. No Gestapo strike force had burst from the shadows. He cast a final glance over his shoulder. Was Albert the stooped old man hawking his meager wares on a ratty blanket? Max supposed it was something else he would never know, and put it out of his mind as he headed up the block to the train station.

TWENTY-SEVEN

The next night was blustery and wet. The temperature hovered just above freezing, and the rain mixed with the icy slush that sluiced through the gutters and turned the sidewalks into minefields of half-frozen puddles.

Max was grateful for his waterproof boots as he splashed down Hardenbergstrasse, a few blocks west of the ruins of the empty Berlin Zoo. He focused on his breathing, trying to break the habit of holding his breath when he was nervous. If he kept that up, he would pass out, and he'd be no good to the resistance sprawled out in the slush.

Hardenbergstrasse was lined with the imposing buildings of the Berlin State School of Fine Arts, its neat architecture largely unmarred by bomb damage. Rain slashed across the classical facades, blurring the buildings into the dusk like a smear of thick paint on a canvas.

Max kept his hands in his pockets, his right palm clutching

his chalk. He had slept poorly last night and dreamed of a dead eye hovering above him. When he jolted awake with a start, the eye had been stuck to the ceiling, gazing pleadingly down at him—and then it had blinked, impossibly slowly, lashes like seaweed moving with languid grace. It wasn't until he woke again into the bruise-colored light of dawn that Max realized he'd had a dream within a dream. All day he'd felt out of sorts and disconnected from himself, as if there were another dream-layer from which he was waiting to wake up.

Past the art school, low-slung apartment blocks presided over a few desultory trees, bare branches dripping and forlorn. Max ducked his head under a skeletal branch and made for a side street of row houses that had collapsed in a pressure blast.

Guess they forgot to open their front doors! he thought crazily.

He found a suitable pile of bricks jutting from the earth like a grave marker and took out his chalk. He wrote the first word of tonight's coded message—*Marta*—and found that the chalk would not leave a mark on the wet brick. He scraped harder and snapped off the tip.

He looked behind him. He couldn't see Gerta through the downpour. He could not see much of anything at all, except the thin limbs of the bare trees.

A shadow changed shape, came toward him quickly, and

then receded, a creature unfurling and then curling into itself. Max's breath caught in his throat. He wiped rain from his eyes.

"Gerta?" he said quietly. His voice was swallowed up by the storm. "Albert?"

The only answer was the dull roar of the rain. For a brief, sweet moment, Max was home in his bed, warm and dry, listening to the murmur of the rain on the roof as he drifted off to sleep. There was no war, no Becker Circle, no dead drop, no Nazi spy.

Uncle Friedrich was alive.

Out of the corner of his eye, the shadows shifted again—a feathery rustling, a great bird spreading its wings. Max's mind raced—the zoo had been bombed months ago, but maybe some animals were still on the loose . . .

He slid his sleeve across his eyes, but it was no use. The rain would not be wiped away.

He wished he had some kind of weapon. He didn't know how to shoot a gun, but even a pocketknife was better than nothing.

He peered into the night—

And then it was upon him. A shadow made whole, screaming and clawing.

He turned to run blindly into the darkness, but the thing gripped his shoulder and spun him around.

"Max!"

It knew his name. He struck out wildly, and it let him go.

"Max, it's me, you idiot!"

He stopped. His pulse was hammering, his vision blurred.

His sister thrust her face into his and screamed at him. "What are you doing?"

"I'm sorry!" he said, swamped with relief. "I thought you were . . ." He stopped himself from saying *a giant bird* or *a shadow monster.*

"It's too wet to write on the bricks!" he said.

She rolled her eyes. "Then find a dry spot!"

Together, they searched the ruins until they came upon a place where the wall had tilted without collapsing. Here, the wreckage had formed a natural shelter from the rain. Quickly, Max chalked the message.

"I think Albert's a crusty old beggar tonight," Gerta said. "Either that or a lady in a fur coat."

"I can't believe we have two more of these to do," Max said as they sloshed back onto Hardenbergstrasse. They were both hopelessly soaked.

"Next time they try to kill Hitler," Gerta said, shivering, "I hope it's summertime."

TWENTY-EIGHT

On the night of the third drop, the moon was a pale shimmer behind the clouds. It was dark and cold, but mercifully dry. Max walked north on Richard-Wagner-Strasse, past the ruins of the opera house, which had been a vast bombed-out shell since an RAF raid scored a direct hit back in November. The moonlight's sallow glow painted the husk of the once-proud building with an eerie phosphorescence, as if it were being lit from within by a single spotlight that refused to go dark.

At the northern edge of the opera house, Max cut across a narrow strip of dead grass. He ducked into a canyon of rubble that was almost sculptural in its ruin—the collapse of the upper balcony had created a cascade of seats twisted and burned into new, unlikely forms. He thought of Frau Becker, and how sad she would be to see such destruction brought to a place of wonder and beauty. And yet there was something oddly beautiful about the way it had all come down, as if in its death throes the opera house had insisted on turning itself into a piece of art.

Beautiful bomb ruins, Max thought, shaking his head. *I am losing my mind.*

He came to a piece of twisted brass that coiled around itself like a snake. Part of a railing, scorched and remade by fire. He kept going, picking through the wreckage of the box seats that had bulged from the sides of the opera house, personal balconies for high-ranking officials and their families, reduced to splinters and tattered velvet curtains.

Beyond the collapsed balconies, there was a forest of marble columns sheared to half their height by the blast. Through the columns, Max could make out a few pedestrians moving down the street. He knew that Gerta was among them. Albert, too, though he would never see the man.

Max chose a column halfway between the street and a collapsed portico whose marble was bone white. He knelt down and placed the tip of the chalk against the column—and froze. There was movement off to his left. An animal? All manner of scavengers prowled the ruins at night, and a place like the opera house made a worthy home for rodents and stray cats.

Max thought of the night before, when he had nearly jumped out of his skin at the sight of his sister. He tried to stay calm. If he let Gerta frighten him again, he would never hear the end of it. He steadied his hand and chalked the coded message: *Heinrich, one day we will see Faust here again.*

As soon as he finished writing, he heard the unmistakable sound of footsteps. Part of the marble floor was still intact, and the sharp clicks echoed between the columns, making it impossible to tell where the footsteps were coming from.

They were definitely not Gerta's.

Albert? he wondered, but didn't dare say the name out loud.

Suddenly Max was blinded by an overwhelming radiance. He put up a hand to shield his face. The forest of columns resounded with footsteps and shouts.

"Hands up!"

"Get on your knees!"

For a brief, weightless moment, Max lost all sense of his body. He saw the scene from above—his slow descent to his knees, the three hulking figures rushing toward him out of the dark with their electric torches blazing.

You and your whole family will die in the camps.

He came back to himself when a massive leather-gloved hand clamped down on his right arm, just beneath his shoulder, and hauled him roughly to his feet. A beam of light shone directly in his eyes. His other senses picked up scattered impressions: the smell of shoe polish and sweat, the sound of self-congratulatory voices.

"—thought he was clever—"

"—such a scrawny little thing—"

"—girl around here somewhere—"

Max's fear was its own universe, blotting out almost everything else, but he managed a thought for Gerta. He hoped she was running into the night, ducking and weaving, escaping . . .

But these men were Gestapo! If they didn't already know who Mutti and Papa were, and where the Hoffmanns lived, they would soon find out. Max had heard stories about how the Gestapo tortured prisoners in the basement cells of their headquarters at Prinz-Albrecht-Strasse 8. "Enhanced interrogation," they called it. Sleep deprivation, starvation, isolation. Whipping, drowning, electrocution.

The rack.

Max's knees gave out, and the Gestapo agent propped him up. He wiggled Max's arms in a perverse dance.

"Look at my Jew-lover puppet!" he said. His comrades laughed.

The agent slammed Max's back against a column. Max's vision swam. The fear that had dulled his wits a moment ago had turned sharply acute, and his mind began to race. There was no slipping out of this huge man's grip, but maybe when they shoved him into the green minna, he could find a way to jump out, hit the ground, roll away . . .

The man lowered his torch. Max blinked. The agent's face

came into focus—surprisingly angular for such a big man, with a jutting chin, a nose that had been broken and reset, and a high forehead. His eyes gleamed as bone white as the ruined portico at his back.

"I am Kriminalkommissar Heller," he said, smiling broadly. "And you're going to tell me where your partner is."

"I don't have a—"

"Uh-uh!" Heller cut him off. "Naughty, naughty. We know she's out here with you. We know she has the documents." He shook Max's arm, bashing him into the column for a second time. Max gasped as the air rushed from his lungs. "We know everything already, so you might as well tell us the truth. I could make things much better for you." He paused. "Or much worse. It's up to you. I really don't care."

Max's body tingled. He felt as if his nerves were live wires.

"I don't have a partner," he said. His voice shook, but he got the words out.

Heller shrugged. "Pity. I was hoping to wrap this up early. Ah, well." He turned to his two fellow agents. The twin red embers of their cigarettes floated in the darkness. "Looks like we've got ourselves a hunt."

Run, Gerta. Max willed her on into the night, far from the clutches of the Gestapo, far from Berlin, far from the war itself . . .

"*Hrrkk.*" With a strangled cry, one of the red embers spun to the ground.

"Hausmann?" Heller said. His grip on Max's arm loosened as he turned to aim his torch at his comrades. At that moment, several things happened at once. As Heller's light swept across the forest of columns, Max saw the prone body of a Gestapo agent lying motionless on the ground. The other agent waved his torch wildly, the beam darting in and out of the columns, illuminating nothing but empty air.

Heller cursed. "Sieg, what is it? What's happened?"

"Hausmann just dropped!" said the second man. "I didn't see anything."

Heller dragged Max toward the fallen agent, shining his beam this way and that. "You're staying with me," he said. Then he nudged Hausmann with the toe of his boot. The man was completely still. His torchlight paused on the man's face. Hausmann's mouth was open, frozen in an expression of shock and pain. A gaping wound in the side of his neck wept blood.

Heller's body tensed. "He's dead. Someone's here."

Sieg cursed. In the torchlight, Max watched Sieg draw his pistol. "Show yourself, you coward!" he cried.

Max's heart raced. *Albert!*

A dark form seemed to glide between the farthest columns, poured like liquid shadow.

"There!" Heller shouted, aiming his torch.

Sieg fired. The *crack* of the pistol split the night, and the bullet took a chunk of marble out of a column.

"There!" Heller shouted again, his voice ragged and nearly hysterical. His beam played across what appeared to be the pinched, sallow face of a young office clerk. Sieg fired again, but the face had already vanished.

Heller swung Max around as he spun in a circle, searching for the figure who was coming out of the dark to strike at them.

There was a shriek of pain. Heller's light darted to the place Sieg had been a moment ago. There was nobody there.

Max felt Heller's grip tighten reflexively. He could smell the man's sour sweat.

"Sieg!" Heller called out. Movement behind them—shuffling, maybe a footstep or two—

Heller spun. And screamed. The figure burst out from behind a column, half running, half falling, as if to embrace the Gestapo agent. Heller let go of Max as he struggled with his attacker. He beat at the back of the figure's head with his heavy torch. Max ducked behind a column and crouched in the shadows. He watched as Heller brutalized the attacker.

Albert is going to die, he thought. *I have to help him.*

But his legs would not carry him out from behind the

column. It was only when the third figure stepped into view that Max realized what had happened.

Albert had shoved Sieg's lifeless body into Heller so that Max could escape.

Heller was fighting with the corpse of his comrade.

In a single smooth motion, the pale, well-dressed "office clerk" glided behind Heller, gripped the man's forehead, yanked his head back, and drew a long knife across his throat.

Heller sputtered. His arms shot out to his sides. The torch clattered to the ground. Albert held him up until Heller's arms dangled and the man stopped twitching. Then he stepped back, and both dead Gestapo agents collapsed in a heap.

In the weird light from the dropped torches, Albert's body heaved and his breath came in gasps.

Max watched him gather himself for a moment. Frau Becker's servant had taken down three Gestapo agents with such ruthless precision, it was jarring to watch him cope with the aftermath.

A hand found his shoulder. Max yelped.

It was Gerta. "We have to stop meeting like this," she said.

"Albert—" Max's voice was hoarse. He swallowed and tried again. "Albert just killed—"

"I know," Gerta said.

Together, they watched Albert slowly relax. His body stilled and his breathing steadied. He stood motionless for a moment, then knelt next to the corpses. With the same efficiency he had just displayed, Albert searched the dead men's pockets, removing their identification and stuffing the papers into his overcoat.

"You'd better be on your way," he said quietly as he opened the third Gestapo agent's coat without looking at Max and Gerta. "Someone will have heard the shots. Police will be here soon."

"Will we see you again?" Max said.

"No," Albert said. "But I'll see you. Now *go*. Tell your parents what happened. They'll know what to do."

With that, Albert clicked off the torches. The forest of columns went dark.

Max and Gerta made their way back through the canyon of fallen balconies in silence. It wasn't until they hurried out onto Richard-Wagner-Strasse that Max was struck by what the Gestapo ambush really meant.

It was the third night of their spy-catching scheme. There was only one person in the Becker Circle (besides Frau Becker herself and Albert) who knew the location of the drop.

They had sniffed out the Nazi spy in their midst.

It was Hans.

TWENTY-NINE

Berlin's majestic Anhalter Station had once been a grand symbol of connection among the people of Europe. From the platforms beneath its great glass-and-steel roof, trains carried thousands of passengers every day to places like Athens and Rome. Now that roof was a skeletal ruin, its glass blown out by incendiary bombs. Whole sections had begun to fall away, and several tracks were pocked with craters. What had once been an international transit hub was reduced to servicing a few local train lines for passengers huddled on the platforms that weren't yet gutted by bombs.

Dawn sent light the color of dirty bathwater down through the open roof. On the walls, shredded propaganda posters displayed a noble, youthful Hitler brandishing a Nazi flag, boldly leading his troops into battle. Nobody moving through Anhalter Station paid them any attention. Everyone was preoccupied. The station might not be of much use to railroad travelers, but the sandbagged shelters of its cavernous interior provided plenty of out-of-the-way nooks and crannies for black-market business.

Hans Meier moved swiftly, keeping his eyes down and his satchel tightly wedged under his armpit. He felt as if he were being propelled by pure nervous energy, floating above the floor tiles.

Perhaps the first clue that the dead drop had been a trap should have been the way Frau Becker mentioned it to him. He had been alone in her sitting room, and it was out of character for the old woman to talk resistance business without other members of the Becker Circle present. She did not like to repeat herself. But Hans didn't think anything of it at the time, and when he got back to his room at the hotel he had called Fritz, his Gestapo handler, and dutifully reported the drop.

That information would be worth at least five hundred Reichsmarks.

Stupid. Hans bit his lip to keep from admonishing himself out loud. He'd gotten too comfortable, that was it. He'd let down his guard.

For more than a year, he'd had it all figured out. He had been a member of the Becker Circle since 1942, welcomed by Frau Becker with open arms thanks to his father's strident anti-Nazi speeches in Zurich. The group trusted him.

After the scattered (and, Hans thought, rather pathetic) 1943 plots on Hitler's life failed, the Gestapo was willing to pay good money for information about future attempts, and even better money for the names of the conspirators. Playing both sides had been easy. Fritz, that ambitious little worm, had practically drooled all over Hans at their first meeting at a beer hall in Unter den Linden, when he learned what kind of information Hans could supply. The trick was not to give the Nazis everything at once—to offer tantalizing clues, a name here and a location there, with the promise of more, always more. That was how you got paid again and again.

What Frau Becker would never understand was that Hans really did hate the Nazis. They were nasty and brutal, and their notions of "racial purity" were pure hogwash from a scientific standpoint. And of course, there were the concentration camps, but Hans never let himself think too hard about those.

So, yes, the Nazis were beneath his contempt. But they paid handsomely for information. He had no doubt that Germany would eventually lose the war—once the Americans landed in France, it would be all over. Before that happened, he intended to take as much of their cash as he could and get out of this whole mess with his head still attached to his neck. Then he would move to the United States—Los Angeles, to be exact. He had pored over American movie magazines. Hollywood after the war was going to be the perfect place for a charming young Swiss gentleman of refined breeding to turn a small fortune into a big one.

In Los Angeles, Hans had read, it was always sunny and warm. You could buy a boat and sail it every day. Not like Lake Geneva in Switzerland, where your boat was stuck in the ice for six months out of the year.

Hans allowed himself to give in to the fantasy. He could almost feel the warm sun on his face, the sand between his toes, the pretty girl on his arm . . .

An announcement for the 6:23 local train interrupted his reverie, bringing him back to frigid Anhalter Station. The voice was garbled and indistinct. The intercom system had been damaged.

There was an upsurge in activity as stragglers hurried toward the platform to catch the train. Hans kept moving toward an abandoned row of caged-in ticket booths, hugging his satchel as if it were his firstborn child.

The satchel was full of cash. Everything he had saved and stashed away that he hadn't dared cross the border with, until today. He no longer had a choice. The Gestapo had paid him a large sum for Frau Becker's name. He'd only betrayed the old woman after much pretend hemming and hawing with Fritz. In truth, he was just waiting for the Gestapo to raise his fee. There was another fat payment for General Vogel. The Nazis reserved a special hatred for traitorous military officers. Hans shuddered to think what the blustery general's fate would be. Guillotined in Plötzensee Prison if he was lucky. More likely, he would be garroted to within an inch of his life, revived, and garroted again while being filmed for Hitler's viewing pleasure.

Hans's satchel also contained a series of smaller payments for reporting the dead drops carried out by Max and Gerta Hoffmann. He didn't like to think too hard about those little bundles of Reichsmarks. He respected the professional abilities of Karl Hoffmann, and thought that Max and Gerta were good kids. But he had to give the Nazis *something*, and he wasn't about to give up Claus von Stauffenberg. If anybody could pull off the assassination of Adolf Hitler, it was the one-eyed officer.

Hans comforted himself during his rare sleepless nights with the thought that, on balance, he was *helping* the resistance. He wasn't a callous man, and he wasn't stupid. Any fool could see that the world would be a better place without the Führer in it. He would never give up Stauffenberg. He hoped he would be lying on a beach in Los Angeles, sipping a cold drink, opening a newspaper to find that the assassination plot had actually succeeded.

He would turn to the girl sunning herself next to him, the fashion model or famous actress, and with a sly grin show her the article. He would say something mysterious to pique her interest, in his gorgeously accented English—*You see, I always knew we would succeed . . .*

Just to the left of the empty ticket booths was an archway that led to what had once been a small restaurant. Its kitchen had been damaged in a raid, and it had never reopened. Fritz would be waiting for him there with his final payment for reporting last night's drop to the Gestapo.

Sure, the whole thing had been a setup. But the way Hans saw it, he'd done his job. Setup or no, the Nazis still owed him money for reporting it.

Inside the shell of the former restaurant, a few of Berlin's homeless were slumped over tables, sleeping on their folded arms.

In the back, a man in a dark trench coat sat draped in shadow. Before him on the small round table was a briefcase. Hans's heart quickened. There was his final payment. He calculated that he would be out of this horribly depressing place in five minutes, his satchel quite a bit heavier, and headed to the Silesian Station, the only station in Berlin still running long-distance trains. With his impeccable Swiss credentials, he would be out of the Reich by nightfall, even with travel as snarled as it was. And with his father's connections, it wouldn't be hard to secure passage from Zurich to America.

The thought of leaving Europe behind gave him a surge of joy. He had spent far too long in this dismal, bombed-out wasteland. It was not the proper environment for a man of his qualities.

He wrinkled his nose at the sour smell that wafted from the dozing vagrants as he moved through the restaurant. He shot a nervous glance over his shoulder—nobody following—and then sat down at Fritz's table.

The Gestapo man's fedora was pulled low, nearly covering his eyes.

"Nice hat," Hans said. "Very stylish."

The Gestapo man did not reply. Hans narrowed his eyes. There was something different about Fritz today. He was a thin, almost waifish man, but today he seemed more substantial, as if he had somehow grown in bulk.

"Anyway," Hans said uneasily. "If you'll kindly slide my fee across the table, I think that will conclude our business. It's been a pleasure; good luck with the war and all that."

Fritz leaned forward, and the shadows receded.

Hans's eyes widened. Before he could react to the sight of the face, the face that was definitely not Fritz—

(*It can't be*)

—a hand shot forward and grabbed Hans's scarf and yanked his head down to the table.

He tried to scream, but his mouth was pressed hard into the briefcase, and the sound that came out was *ggrrrhhhhmmmmm*.

"Death to Nazi scum," said a soft voice in his ear.

"Albert," he tried to say, "wait—"

The blade entered the base of his neck, and his whole body went cold. It felt impossibly long, an icy needle slicing up through his spine. There was very little pain—just a numbness that blossomed quickly. He tried to fight but found that he could not move his arms or legs.

He tasted rust in his mouth, and then he was on a beach, but the sun was cold on his skin (*how strange*) and the girl on his arm was nothing but sand. A chill wind kicked up and blew her away, and Hans found that he was alone, holding on to nothing but empty air. Then the sun set in a flash and the beach went dark.

THIRTY

The door of the beautiful row house on Perleberger Strasse, with its brass gargoyle knocker, was heavy and locked. But it was still no match for the battering ram the four Gestapo agents kept in the back of their green minna.

They announced themselves once, and when nobody answered (no surprise there), they smashed the door off its hinges. Inside the front hall, one agent stood guard to prevent escape, marveling at the odd portraits that lined the walls. This woman was supposed to be a crazy old bird, and judging by her ancestors, that was no exaggeration. Another agent searched the coatroom and, finding it empty, drew his pistol and went upstairs to the second floor. The remaining two agents moved aside the velvet curtain at the end of the hallway.

There, inside a sumptuous sitting room, they found a stooped old woman wearing a furry Russian hat feeding papers into a roaring fire in the massive fireplace. They screamed for her to stop. She tossed a final crumpled page into the flames and turned around, leaning heavily on her cane.

One agent drew his gun to cover his comrade while he crossed the room to apprehend the old woman.

The fire raged at her back. She smiled and pointed her cane at the man, halting his approach. There was a chance the cane could be disguising a weapon of some sort—like the Jews they loved so much, the resistance thrived on unfair advantages and dirty tricks.

"In the end," she said, "your hatred will be your undoing. The world will know what you have done, and the human race will not stand for it."

The Gestapo agent said nothing. He had heard all manner of pleas, invocations, promises, and threats from the criminals, spies, and traitors he had taken prisoner over the years. At least this was just one old woman. Last night, three of his comrades on a stakeout at the opera house had been murdered by what must have been an entire gang of resistance fighters.

When he realized that her cane wasn't about to shoot at him, he took another step toward her and reached for the cuffs attached to his belt.

"Death to Hitler!" she shouted in an astonishingly loud

voice. The Gestapo agent rolled his eyes. He had heard that one before, too.

The woman's hand moved as if she were popping a piece of candy into her mouth. With a gleam in her eyes, she bit down hard on something. The Gestapo agent cursed and rushed to catch her as she crumpled to the ground. He knelt with her head in his lap and wrenched open her jaw with his fingers.

Foam erupted from her mouth and gathered about her lips. He probed for the capsule, but it had already dissolved, releasing its deadly cyanide poison. The old woman twitched once in his arms and went still.

The agent closed his eyes. He could feel a stress headache coming on. His boss was not going to be happy. The old woman was the ringleader of this resistance group, and he had been commanded to take her alive.

His only hope was that when the Führer heard about this failure, his name was left out of the report.

THIRTY-ONE

ake only what you can fit in a small bag!" Mutti yelled upstairs.

Max shoved his soccer cleats into his knapsack, then changed his mind. He tossed them away and added another sweater from his drawer. He was trying to think practically. Underwear, pants, shirts. He would wear two coats and a scarf. He glanced at his shelf, hesitated, then swept all of his medieval figurines into the bag and cinched it shut.

The Hoffmanns were going to a safe house. When Max heard the term *safe house*, he imagined a fortress with battlements, a moat, and a drawbridge. But he knew that in reality, their new home would be a cramped, nondescript flat where they could hide out, in a neighborhood where people kept to themselves.

He went to his window. A gorgeous morning had emerged from a cold gray dawn—clear blue sky, with a hint of wispy clouds on the horizon. He had not slept a wink. After Max and Gerta got home and told their parents about the compromised drop, Hans's betrayal, and Albert's vicious attack on the Gestapo agents, Papa and Mutti had not hesitated before announcing that it was time to leave the villa. They could never come back home. There was no telling how much information Hans had fed to the Nazis.

It was time for the surviving members of the resistance to go even deeper underground. It was time to hide.

Max looked down at the street, half expecting gleaming black cars to screech to a halt in front of their house, Gestapo agents and SS men and maybe even Hitler himself to rush up the front porch. He rubbed his eyes. He was still running on adrenaline. His heart hadn't stopped hammering since they'd fled the opera house.

He remembered staring out of this window at squadrons of RAF planes while distant fires splashed crimson across the low clouds.

He remembered a time before the war when his uncle Friedrich had pointed out constellations in the night sky, Orion's Belt and the five bright stars of Cassiopeia.

He remembered the day his mother had put up the green curtains. He lingered for a moment, his hand on the thin, silky fabric, before he bid his bedroom goodbye.

In the hall, he met Gerta. Her bag was slung across her shoulder.

"You know what the worst part is?" she said. "Picturing all their grubby Nazi fingers poking through our stuff. I think it would be better if we burned it down."

"You want to burn our house down?"

"It's not our house anymore, Maxi." She gestured at the walls. "This isn't our life anymore. We gotta get used to that—fast."

Max followed his sister downstairs. Papa and Mutti were waiting in the sitting room.

"Did you talk to Frau Becker?" Max asked.

"No," Papa said. "It isn't safe."

"Do you think she's okay?" Gerta said.

"I think she will never let the Gestapo capture her," Mutti said. "And neither will we. Now come. Get your coats."

"I never thought it would be Hans," Max said, putting on his light jacket, then his heavy overcoat. It still didn't seem real. Now the thought of Hans's Swiss chocolates made him sick. "Why did he do it?"

"We'll never know," Mutti said with a bitter edge to her voice. "Maybe he's a true Nazi sympathizer. Maybe he just likes money. Maybe he did it for some Aryan *fräulein*."

Max glanced around the sitting room, trying to etch the sight of the furniture and the wallpaper into his mind. He had always taken his house for granted—the sofa was here, the armchair there—but now he wished he could run his hands along every banister and lampshade, to sit at the kitchen table over a bowl of hot stew one last time.

"We knew this day might come," Papa said. "But just because we're leaving our house, it doesn't mean we don't have a home. Home is wherever we are—the four of us. Never forget that."

Max went to the door.

"No, Maxi—not that way," Papa said. "I think it's best if we go out the back."

Max followed his parents and sister through the kitchen, out the back door, and into the small garden behind the house. They moved through some tall weeds that had survived the frost, opened the gate in the fence, and slipped into the narrow alley that separated their backyard from the neighbor's.

Max used to play here before the war, but over the past few years, he had nearly forgotten its existence. As the Hoffmanns moved quickly down the alley, Gerta gave him a nudge.

"Look." She pointed to a clot of dead scrub brush and brambles that seemed to grow out of the bottom of the fence. Suspended in the thorny twigs was the painted figure of a prince, his silver crown chipped, his tunic faded.

Max snatched it up and put it in his pocket. He tried to remember the day he had dropped it back here, but he could not. He imagined that it was bright and sunny, that the world was peaceful, and that he was happy.

"Hurry," Papa said, and Max ran to catch up.

AUTHOR'S NOTE

Many of the characters in this book, along with the events and interactions that make up their day-to-day lives, are fictional. However, the bomb-ravaged cityscape of 1943–1944 Berlin was a very real place, the backdrop against which the real plot to kill Hitler—Operation Valkyrie—took shape.

The plotters of the Becker Circle are fictional, but their jobs, experiences, and beliefs reflect the real-life members of the Valkyrie conspiracy, which consisted of anti-Nazi army officers, aristocrats, intellectuals, businessmen, diplomats, and—yes—a certain Russian émigrée princess. Their activities on behalf of Berlin's Jewish population are based on the work of the real-life Solf Circle, a group of dissidents who met at a Berlin salon and were eventually betrayed by a Swiss doctor.

Claus von Stauffenberg, the lynchpin of the conspiracy, really did sustain horrific injuries in North Africa, courtesy of an American fighter-bomber. Even with one eye and three working fingers—a disability he regarded as a minor inconvenience—Stauffenberg was by all accounts a commanding presence, a brilliant leader, and a staunch anti-Nazi. Unlike the vast majority of his colleagues, he never joined the Nazi party, and wasn't shy about telling friends and colleagues that he was in full revolt against Hitler, calling the Führer "evil incarnate." As a secret plotter, he played a dangerous game— and yet, as one of the most promising young officers in the Wehrmacht, he seems to have blinded potential foes with his talent and charisma, and was afforded the privilege and access he needed to carry out his plans. I am indebted to the book *Secret Germany* by Michael Baigent and Richard Leigh, which explores his life and the Valkyrie conspiracy in great detail.

Princess Marie is heavily inspired by the real-life Marie Vassiltchikov, a young Russian princess who lived in Berlin during the war, worked in the German Foreign Office, and had an insider's view of the plot to kill Hitler as it developed. I would recommend her book *Berlin Diaries, 1940–1945* to anyone who wants to learn more about life in Berlin during the rise and fall of the Third Reich. Her diary was an invaluable resource, and I drew upon her memories for many details in this book, from the tiger's whiskers assassination scheme to the chalk inscriptions on bombed-out houses.

Wherever possible, I tried to situate the lives of the Hoffmanns in the midst of historical upheaval using real dates and places. Regarding some of the major milestones, November 1943 really did mark a drastic escalation in RAF bombing raids. The "fashion show" assassination was a real plan, and Hitler actually did cancel his appearance at the last minute without giving a reason. By this point in time—February 1944—the Führer had survived many attempts on his life through sheer luck, including one involving bombs hidden in two liquor bottles stashed aboard his aircraft. The bombs failed to detonate.

For a wealth of details about the daily lives of Berliners during the war, credit goes to *Berlin at War* by Roger Moorhouse. This book provided the inspiration for countless moments in the Hoffmanns' lives. Proper air-raid procedure, the wartime rationing system, tactics of the Gestapo, the texts of radio broadcasts (though *Hornet and Wasp* is sadly fictional)—I learned so much from this book, and I'm grateful to its author for his exhaustive research.

Finally, any liberties I've taken with the geography of Berlin or the sequences of historical events are mine alone. If I bent certain situations (and city streets!) to the whims of this story, it's no fault of the authors mentioned above.

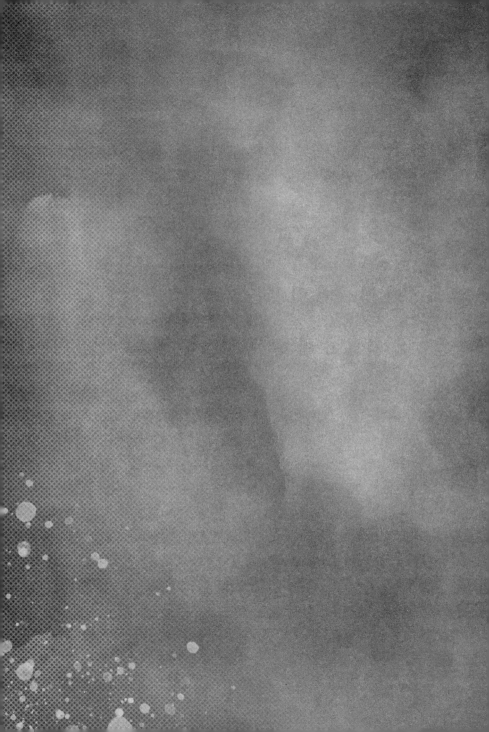

ABOUT THE AUTHOR

Andy Marino was born and raised in upstate New York, and currently lives in New York City with his wife and two cats. You can visit him at andy-marino.com.